THE LEDGER

JOHN NETTI

Black Rose Writing | Texas

The author grants the final approval for this literary material.

First printing

This is a work of fiction. Names, characters, businesses, places, events, and incidents are either the products of the author's imagination or used in a fictitious manner. Any resemblance to actual persons, living or dead, or actual events is purely coincidental.

ISBN: 978-1-68513-208-8
PUBLISHED BY BLACK ROSE WRITING
www.blackrosewriting.com

Printed in the United States of America
Suggested Retail Price (SRP) $19.95

The Ledger is printed in EB Garamond

*As a planet-friendly publisher, Black Rose Writing does its best to eliminate unnecessary waste to reduce paper usage and energy costs, while never compromising the reading experience. As a result, the final word count vs. page count may not meet common expectations.

A special thank you to Megan, my writing coach, and Anne-Marie, who shared her professional insights. Thank you to the beta readers, Gary, Susan, Pat, Fran, Molly, Denise, Nichole, Jean-Marie, John, Holly, Maria, Kim, Sue, and Donna; your feedback significantly improved the story. Thank you to my wife, Jean, for putting up with my long absences in the writing room. To my children, David and Laura, and my grandchildren, Alexis and Tyler, you are always there for me. Finally, I want to thank you, God, for the gift of writing.

THE LEDGER

"Rage, rage against the dying of the light."

–Dylan Thomas

CHAPTER 1

Maddy Reynolds
October 1991

Who the hell was that guy? The redhead had watched her from the gift shop as she checked her luggage, and when she walked to her gate, he followed. Waiting to board, she turned, and he gazed at her from a distance with his arms folded. She was in the air, watching rain beading up on the window, wondering if the redhead had been tailing her or if she was paranoid. *I'm just jumpy,* she thought. *I've been too far away from people, and for too long.*

City lights glistened, the night looked raw, and she watched the humanity below undulating like boiling lava. Maddy knew its violence well; four times, it had almost killed her. She wondered why she had accepted the invitation, but deep down, she knew. She needed to move on.

Finding peace in secluded Berry Lake, making a few friends, and even falling in love helped her through the last three years, but she knew she couldn't hide forever.

The invitation to speak at the conference had arrived in August, and she hadn't tossed it out. She had taped it to the refrigerator, ignored it, and filled out the response at the last minute. Slipping it into the envelope, she had driven it to the post office and sat in her Jeep, trying to decide what to do. She knew dropping it into the box meant opening herself to the wiles of the world again. Whether it was her inner voice that had prodded her, or maybe her better self, it didn't matter, because she was in the air and on her way.

After the Cupid nightmare, Maddy had thought the mountains were her ticket to a serene life, but she was wrong. *Oh, sweet elusive peace, how I craved you, but you weren't meant to be.* Instead, Avery Jordan and his brainchild, The Glades, had awaited. Nestled on a mountain across the lake from her new home, the vast compound had ravaged the souls of innocents, condemning them to lives of sex slavery. *Little did I know,* she thought, looking at occasional streetlights in darkness as the plane drifted over the countryside.

I was living the life I had hoped for and not the life that was. She felt foolish about her self-deceit back then. The great fire that consumed The Glades brought reality crashing down. Since then, she had kept the world at bay, letting in only a trusted few, including the love of her life, Adam.

They met the night of the fire. A bond formed, and she let him into her heart. Trusting men didn't come easy after her divorce from Jack; the betrayal of his affair had cut her deep. Adam was grieving his wife's death and needed time, too. They took things slowly, gave each other space, and were patient. In time, Maddy found the only happiness with a man she'd ever known.

The engines whistled, the plane thumped as it hit the ground, and a blast from reversing turbines roared, forcing her forward in her seat. She'd arrived in the nation's capital, and the redhead faded into the back of her mind.

She shuffled out of the crowded airplane, rolled the carry-on to the taxi area, and hailed a cab. "Where to, lady?" the cabbie wearing a Yankees cap backward asked.

"The Hyatt Regency on Capitol Hill." She hopped in, and the kid inquired if she was in town on business. "I'm here to speak at a conference."

"What's it about?" When she said 'serial killers,' he asked if she was a psychiatrist.

"No, I was a detective and worked a case a while back."

"Wow, that's heavy. Was it any of the biggies?"

"Cupid." His face lit up.

"Man, he was the worst. Did you ever meet the guy?"

Not wanting to share that she had killed the maniac, she said, "Sort of."

The cab sped through the rainy blackness, and headlights glistened on more cars than she had seen in three years. Her mind returned to the night in a stone quarry when she had faced off with a man she thought was her friend. He had worked his way into her life to kill her. Cupid was Maddy's first lesson in cunning deceit, and nothing had been the same since.

The taxi pulled beneath the overhang, and a bellhop came out to take her bag. She handed the driver a credit card, and handing it back, he stared as if she were Muhammad Ali. "You're Maddy Reynolds?" She turned her back to the gawking cabbie and entered the lobby.

She got to her room a little after nine o'clock. Tired and aching from sitting cramped up for three hours, she tossed her bag on the bed and ran hot water in the tub. She undressed, glimpsed herself in the mirror, and winced. Deformed flesh from two gunshot wounds and scars from a knife reminded her of the trail of woes that had sent her into seclusion. Though considered beautiful by most men, Maddy felt ugly at the sight of her damaged body. *I can't believe Adam desires me as much as he does.*

She stepped into the soothing warmth, laid back, and let her mind drift like a sailboat on Berry Lake. Perfection was a summer day on beautiful Berry Lake. The Adirondack Mountains had taught her to connect with nature in ways she hadn't known were possible. Growing up in Chicago and Utica, New York, she was unaware of a void within her until the ancient hills, trees, and lakes opened her mind to the new reality.

She slipped into a robe and dried her hair with a towel when she stepped out of the tub. The message light on the phone blinked, and she pushed the button. 'Hello, Ms. Reynolds; this is Gerald Ellis. I have something vital to discuss while you're in Washington. It's unrelated to the conference you're attending. Please meet me tomorrow during your session's lunch break at Trilogies, the coffee shop across the street from the hotel. Just have a seat, and I'll find you. See you then.' *Strange, I don't know a Gerald Ellis,* she thought as she jotted a note on her itinerary.

Maddy got comfortable in sweat clothes and unwound. She switched off the lights and brought the phone to a chair near a window overlooking the city. When she dialed Adam, he answered. "Hi, babe," she said, feeling his warmth and missing him already.

"I was hoping you hadn't forgotten me." Adam sounded exhausted.

"How can I forget you after last night?" Maddy was thinking of their night of goodbye lovemaking. They both sighed, and he said he wished he was with her. "Will I see you this week?" she asked.

"I got a call tonight not to make any plans. I'm being placed on a special assignment tomorrow."

"Aww, honey," she whined.

"I know. Let's hope it won't be for too long. I'll leave you a message when I find out about my situation."

She closed her eyes and felt a pang of pain, knowing the danger he faced whenever he went undercover. She asked him to stay safe before hanging up. Gazing at the bustling traffic and the Washington Monument towering in the distance, she felt something moving inside. The gnawing sensation that someone she loved was being drawn away to an unknown fate was a feeling she'd had before. Maddy wouldn't let her mind go there and instead thought about lying before a fire with Adam again.

CHAPTER 2

Maddy reviewed her presentation on serial killers the following morning in the hotel lounge. As she perused the conference material, she noticed all the panelists except for her were academics. *Great. I'll be a fish out of water.* She wasn't the academic type. They pitched her as having hands-on experience with an active psychopathic killer, and although she wasn't a natural public speaker and never pretended to be an expert in anything, she was sure of what she knew about the criminal mind. She had paid a high price for that knowledge and wasn't afraid to tell her story.

By the time she found the room where the meeting was to be held, people had gathered around the coffee and Danish. She dropped her shoulder bag at her place at the front table and headed for the food. A voice called out as she returned to the table with a cup of coffee. She turned, and Sidney Myers followed with full hands, smiling. When she first met the criminal psychologist years earlier, Maddy thought he was obnoxious, but he took a liking to her and worked to win her friendship.

"Sidney, how are you?"

"Better. Now that I know someone is here, who knows what the hell they're talking about." She laughed, thinking no one ever had to wonder what was on his mind; it was what she liked about him.

When they reached the table, he switched name tags to sit next to her. "So, tell me, Sidney, why are serial killers such a hot topic? I can't believe the people here."

"Because we expect more like them. The social fabric of our society is breaking down. You know: the family, religion, traditions. These are not just stodgy old notions meant to give us the illusion of mom and apple pie. They are meaningful constructs that ground civilizations. The serial killers we know of are only the most visible who've fallen off the grid; we expect to see many others like them." He turned his attention to her and asked how she'd been since that horrific night when The Glades burned.

She sat back in her chair, smirked, and recalled the first time she met Sidney. He had tried to pry his way into her head, asking questions about her father's murder and psychoanalyzing her motivation for becoming a detective. "You're not doing your Sigmund Freud routine on me again, are you?"

He laughed and said he only did that with pretty young detectives on their first cases. "I'm serious; how have you been since that night? It must have been traumatic." He had put his wise-ass self to the side and looked at her with authentic concern. She said she was still coming out of her cave. Sidney was a brilliant psychologist, and she knew at that moment he saw the sadness she worked to keep hidden.

"I must tell you, that book you sent me made a real difference. I struggled to understand why I kept going toe-to-toe with depraved killers. Your chapter on the changing faces of evil and the people called to fight it helped a lot. You're a pretty deep thinker when you're not being a dick." He placed his hand on hers and laughed a loud belly laugh; people looked over. His insight about evil had moved her. He believed it changes and appears in a distinctly different form once recognized.

He kept his hand on hers and looked into her eyes. "You're special, Maddy. You don't realize how special you are." She frowned, not believing him, but nodded.

The crowd quieted as Marcia Haskins, the program coordinator, stood at the podium and asked for everyone's attention. Sidney leaned over and whispered, "I hope you brought plenty of NoDoz to stay awake."

Marcia thanked everyone for coming. She talked about the critical work they did, then went right into the political significance of their topic.

"As we sit here, just down the street at the Capitol, our leaders are debating the further deterioration of our social fabric with growing concern."

Sidney tilted his head and smiled. "I told you."

"The mind of a serial killer is today's topic," Haskins continued. "It is only one of many social ills that need addressing. Senators and congressional representatives are watching our organization's work today and in the future. They believe if we don't provide meaningful solutions and mental illness continues to metastasize, there will be unthinkable consequences in the future."

Haskins said they had a full agenda, then introduced Dr. Lisa Downer, chairperson of Behavioral Psychology at New York University. They slated Maddy to speak in the last session at three o'clock, but she felt she'd heard three different versions of how the psychopathic mind functioned before the 11:30 lunch break.

As others went to the dining area, she stepped outside to meet Gerald Ellis at Trilogies. Before entering the upscale café, she noticed a crowd gathered around the middle of an intersection. She walked over, and a man in his thirties lay sprawled in the street, blood oozing from his ears; his eyes were wide open. She had seen that look several times and knew the guy was dead.

Not feeling much like eating, she sat in a booth in the restaurant, ordered a Coke, and waited. When it neared 12:45 and Ellis hadn't shown up, she paid the check and started back to the conference.

Wondering if the guy in the street had been Ellis, she plodded along through the rest of the presented material as her mind kept returning to the lifeless eyes staring into the sky. She occasionally laughed at the not-very-flattering comments that Sidney whispered about a few of the presenters. It surprised her when Marcia returned to the podium, interrupting Dr. Patrick Parks's presentation on unresolved oedipal rage near the end of the agenda. It seemed rude when the woman asked for everyone's attention.

"I'm sorry to interrupt Dr. Parks's fascinating discussion, but we have a special guest, and I'm sure he won't mind. Cynthia Morgan, Senator Steven Winthrop's assistant, has taken time from her busy schedule at the Capitol to say a few words."

Dr. Parks huffed off the stage as a plain woman with Coke-bottle-thick glasses and shoulder-length, spaghetti-straight hair stepped up and bubbled out her message. "When Senator Winthrop heard this group was in town, he insisted one of his staff be present to convey his full support for your work."

Is Senator Winthrop interested in serial killers?

"The Senator believes serial killers are bellwethers for what's coming if the proper policies, infrastructure, and services are not in place." Maddy gave Sidney a quizzical look as he whispered, "This senator must be a real forward thinker; it's encouraging."

Morgan spent the next hour expounding Senator Winthrop's accomplishments, but Maddy realized it was a campaign blurb for his upcoming reelection. When Morgan left the room, it was 3:45, leaving Maddy only fifteen minutes to present. She folded her notebook, figuring there wasn't enough time, but Sidney piped up as Marcia Haskins returned to the platform, and he insisted Maddy Reynolds speak for the remaining time. Marcia said, "Of course."

Although not prepared to speak impromptu, Maddy set aside her presentation, and as she took the podium, she wondered what she could say in a few minutes that might make a difference.

"I will share a few words about what I know of serial killers." She looked out at the faces. A few people were writing, others looked at their watches, and three or four, including Sidney, were paying close attention. She continued, "Call to mind a dear friend, someone you've known for years. He's proven trustworthy, been to your home, met your spouse and children; your family adores him." The audience seemed to play along for a bit.

"Now, imagine you drop by his house to pick up a book he wishes to lend you. While you wait for him to find it in another room, you open the door to what you think is his study. You step inside and see several pairs of little girls' underwear on a wall. On another wall, someone placed newspaper clippings about murdered girls. Photos of children bound alive and the same children, dead, are side by side and stacked one over the next like diplomas from prestigious universities."

She peered out, and the audience looked like they were crashing to Earth on Space Mountain. "You feel your throat tighten, your knees are weak, and you can't move. Your heart pounds so hard you think you might pass out. Sweat beads up on your forehead. You lean your hand on a desk to get your bearing, then start for the door, but it's too late. Your friend is glaring at you."

"Too petrified to scream, you freeze. The face of the loving man you thought you knew fills with rage. His eyes are bulging; the veins on his neck and forehead are popping out so far you think they might burst. He walks to you, and the last things you see are his hate-filled eyes and the glitter of the knife he's thrusting into your heart. That's what I know of serial killers."

There was silence. Maddy stepped down, looked at Sidney, and gestured as if to say, 'I tried.' He stood up and clapped, and a handful of others followed suit. She was rushing to catch her flight, but the room exploded with applause before she walked out.

She ran to the lobby, and as she checked out of the hotel, she saw a stack of newspapers on the counter. "Are these recent?" she asked.

"They just arrived; help yourself," the woman at the front desk said. She grabbed one, went outside the hotel, and hopped into a cab. *Boy, am I glad that's over.* Sighing, looking at the traffic, she wondered if she'd make her flight. Opening the evening paper, she started scanning headlines, and when she reached the local news, she read Gerald Ellis, Assistant to Congressional Representative Herman Suarez, Killed in Hit and Run. *That was him.*

The article said that a black Cadillac sped off after hitting Ellis. At 11:20 that morning, he tried to cross the street near the Hyatt Regency. There was little additional information, only that police were investigating the incident and that his parents survived him.

She dropped the paper on her lap and thought of the blank stare on the young man's face. Looking out at the traffic, an old feeling returned.

Something involving her was happening, and she didn't know what it was. That feeling had plagued her three years earlier as The Glades sucked her into its web of deceit and perversity.

What can this mean? Her mind raced. *Maybe it was an accident, but in broad daylight? And the car was a Cadillac? It sounds suspicious as hell.* She tried to recall the guy's message. *He sounded serious and had something vital to discuss. He worked for a congressional representative; what the hell is going on? I've been off the map for three years; how could I be a source of interest to anyone?*

Plagued with questions as her cab let her out at the airport, she went to her gate with her mind buzzing as if she had drunk a gallon of high-octane coffee. With her flight delayed, she sat with her arms crossed, waiting. When the plane boarded, and she handed her pass to the attendant, she glanced around and the guy with the red hair was standing last in line. *Son of a bitch!*

She stepped out of line and started back to confront him. He saw her and bolted. Maddy stood dumbfounded as he disappeared into a throng of people. *What the hell is going on? Who is that guy?* She got on the plane and sat in the last row, wondering why she'd come to the conference. *I didn't even get to make my presentation.*

The plane filled, but the redhead didn't appear. *I can't believe this is happening again,* she thought, feeling the way she did years earlier when The Glades mystery unfolded.

It was a direct flight from Dulles to Syracuse, and her mind reeled the entire time in the air. She tried to determine if she'd been out of touch so long her imagination had gotten the best of her or if she had stepped into something she didn't understand.

When the plane landed, she went to the stand outside the gate and told the flight attendant she had talked to a man who lent her a book before she boarded. "He went to the restroom and missed the flight. Can you give me the name of the person who missed the flight? I'd like to return the novel."

The flight attendant looked at her and smiled as though she didn't believe a word of the story. "Sure, honey, I think I get it. His name is David

L. Peterson, and he's from Scranton. That's all I can give you. Good luck." She wrote it down and looked up, and the woman winked.

The wheels of her luggage spun over concrete, echoing through the dim airport parking garage on her way to her Jeep. There was no one around, and she wished she had her weapon. She always felt vulnerable when she didn't have a handgun. Becoming a High Master Shooter during her teenage years was her way of dealing with anxiety after her father's murder. It still worked for her whenever she felt threatened.

She found her Jeep, made it out of the dungeon-like garage, and started north on Route 81 toward Watertown, the fastest route to Berry Lake. An hour and a half into the three-hour drive, she passed Fort Drum and finally relaxed. When she reached the long dark road through mountains, it was like Valium to her soul. The further she drove, the further Ellis and the redhead drifted into the background.

Until she left her mountain home, she didn't realize how much living a secluded life had grown on her. The blackness of night and occasional glimpses of a full moon through the pines brought her to a peaceful place. After three years, the woods, mountains, and lakes had become part of her, and she couldn't imagine living elsewhere.

When she turned off Route 3 onto the road up the mountain to her place, the gravel crunching beneath the tires was like a sweet song. She pulled up, and the house was lit up just as she'd left it. *I'm home.*

CHAPTER 3

Maddy slept late the following day. She rolled over in bed a few times, covering her head with a pillow, blocking the sun, and hiding from the world. The wheels turned, her brain kicked into gear, and Gerald Ellis's voice on the hotel phone played back in her head: *I have something vital to discuss with you.* She thought of him lying in the street, then the strange guy who had stalked her. She threw the covers off and sat up. *Shit! I knew I should have stayed home.*

She slid into sweat clothes and started a pot of coffee. Berry Lake glittered below as Maddy sat looking out the kitchen window of her home atop the mountain. It was a crisp October morning, and the sun played hide-and-seek with a few low-hanging clouds. Boats moved on the water, and the brilliant red, orange, and yellow trees on the humpback mountains created a tapestry of colors, reminding her of why she loved the life she'd been living. It was fall in the Adirondacks, and it was beautiful.

A rusted station wagon crunched its way up the road to her house, and a heavyset woman got out. It was Rose, the server from Lena's Diner. Smiling, she waved. She waddled up to the deck, carrying a glass tray covered with tinfoil. "Hi, dear." She gave Maddy a one-handed hug. "I'm so glad you're back. I made a blueberry cobbler for you."

Rose was a cherished friend. She had given Maddy comfort the night of the fire when she lay in the street, slashed up with knife wounds after her battle with The Glades's enforcer, Sedgwick Neri. "Come inside; I have coffee on." As she readied the morning brew, Rose sat and started catching her up on the latest goings-on around town.

"Lester's wife Marjorie stopped by the diner yesterday, and did she have a tale to tell. Lester is lucky to be alive." She leaned over, reached for the tinfoil cover, and pulled it off the dish, exposing the cobbler. She took an already sliced piece and placed it on a plate Maddy had set before her.

"Last Tuesday, Marjorie put a garbage bag on the back porch for him to take to the bin when he got home. That was about three o'clock in the afternoon, but it was dark when he had dinner and a few beers."

Rose pushed the cobbler closer to Maddy, encouraging her to take some before she ate it all. "So, Lester takes the bag and heads behind the barn, with Luke, his German Shepard, following along. He hears breaking glass, metal clanking, and sounds like two cars crashing inside the barn. Lester freezes, and Luke takes off, running into the barn."

On her third piece of cobbler, Rose held up her mug, and Maddy filled it with coffee, wishing she would get to the point. "Now, where was I?" Rose's failing memory was an idiosyncrasy Maddy tolerated in her friend, and she reminded her where she was in her story.

"Oh, yeah, there was a roar, and an ear-piercing yelp, in the barn, and the poor man was so scared he couldn't move. A ghostly black figure appeared in the doorway, and Lester couldn't tell what it was. But when it stood up, he said it was the biggest black bear he'd ever seen."

Rose's chubby cheeks reddened; she breathed rapidly, sweat beaded on her forehead as though she were standing in the barnyard herself. She took a sip of coffee and added, "The bear started toward him, growling. His teeth were showing, and he twisted his head like something pissed him off. Lester was too terrified to move, and according to Marjorie, that's when he lost his bowels." *Oh, geez, I wish she didn't tell me that*, Maddy thought as she put her piece of cobbler back on her plate.

"Marjorie went to the door. She saw what was going on and ran for Lester's shotgun. She unloaded both barrels into the beast, and it took off."

Maddy wanted to know what had happened to the dog. "Poor Luke's head was near torn off. Lester's heart broke about it."

Rose stared into the air, nibbling on the cobbler, lost in thought for a moment before continuing. "Lester had a freezer in the barn stocked with fish he'd caught and some venison from last hunting season. He thinks he left the door ajar, and when the bear got a whiff of the fish and meat, that's what happened. Never tempt a hungry bear with food."

"I thought black bears were only dangerous to humans if you bother their cubs," Maddy said.

"That's what I thought too, but Andy, the game warden, told Lester that's a misconception. It's true for brown bears, but for black bears, it's the hungry males to watch out for, and that's what Lester was facing."

"I better keep my garbage locked down." Rose nodded in agreement.

"According to Andy, this bear is intelligent, massive, and has damaged at least five homes in the area. He thinks we haven't seen the last of him."

The two women sat silently before Rose brought up a more sensitive subject. "Are you planning on attending The Glades Memorial dedication Friday?"

Maddy looked at the mountain across the lake where The Glades once stood. She could see the shiny new granite memorial gleaming in the morning light. Deep in thought, her mind went to the horrific fire that burned the place down. "I might want to go." Rose put her hand on hers, knowing she might be thinking of Hector, the boy who started the inferno and died that night.

"We can go together if you'd like."

"I think Hector would like that," Maddy said. She had developed a tender spot for the boy from the moment she had met him. He projected toughness, but she saw through his crusty veneer. It covered the pain he'd endured growing up with an alcoholic father. Like Maddy, Hector grew up before he was ready, and also like her, he learned the world had little sympathy for the woes of a wounded child.

When Rose stood, Maddy walked out with her. "Don't forget to keep your garbage covered," Rose said, smiling as she drove off.

Returning to the kitchen, she started tidying up. The phone rang. "Hello." When there was no response, she asked who it was.

"Is this Maddy Reynolds?" the voice of a young woman with an Asian accent asked.

"Yes."

"You need to help me."

"Who is this?" A click and a dial tone followed.

"Shit!" she shouted, realizing she shouldn't have asked the girl her name. She wrote the caller ID on an envelope and called back, but there was no answer. "Damn!"

Gerald Ellis and the redheaded guy popped into her head, and she realized something was going on she didn't yet understand. It made no sense to ignore it. She contacted Directory Assistance for the DC area and got Herman Suarez's phone number, the congressman Ellis had worked for. They gave her two, one in Washington and the other in New Mexico, his home state. She dialed the Washington number, and a woman answered.

"I'd like to speak with Congressman Suarez."

"Are you a New Mexico resident?"

"I'm from New York, but I have something critical to discuss with him."

"If you give me your name and number, he'll get back to you, but it may take a few weeks." Frustrated, she gave the information, and after a long silence, the woman asked her to hang on. Maddy realized the assistant recognized her name, and when she returned to the phone, she put her through to the congressman.

"Hello, Ms. Reynolds; this is Herman Suarez."

"Congressman, I have something important to discuss, but before I do, I need to understand how you know me?"

"I can't tell you that."

He can't fucking tell me that? She sighed, then explained that one of his staff had contacted her two nights ago and asked to meet for lunch. "He had something vital to discuss but was killed in a very suspicious hit-and-run accident fifteen minutes before the meeting. I'd like to know what Mr. Ellis wanted to talk about."

"Gerald was a dear friend and an important member of my team. He was gathering information for a congressional probe. We have not made it public, so I can't give you any more beyond that, but I assure you, we'll be back in touch. Ms. Reynolds, we believe you have important information we will need. I'm sorry I can't tell you more. Stay safe." He hung up.

Stay safe? Flummoxed, Maddy stared at the phone, listening to the dial tone. *Aww, man, what am I into now?* She hung up and noticed the light on the message machine blinking. It was from Adam, who must have called while she was speaking with Suarez.

"Hi, honey, it's me. There is bad news. I'll be incognito for at least a couple of weeks. I was lucky I could make this call. I'm missing you and will think of our last night together. Love you."

Maddy plopped onto the sofa, deflating like a gouged tire with its air rushing out. As an investigator for the New York State Police, she knew whenever he used the term incognito, it meant he was going undercover.

She shook her head, thinking about how things could go sideways without warning. *Today is Tuesday. It was only Saturday when Adam and I lay in front of the fireplace without care. Now he's gone for who knows how long. Plus, something is flitting outside my world, waiting to come crashing through; I feel it.*

She focused on her situation and turned her attention to the red-haired guy. She went to her purse and fished out the slip of paper the flight attendant had given her. She called information in Scranton, Pennsylvania, but there was no listing for David L. Peterson. On a hunch, she contacted the obituaries at the Scranton Times and found David Lawrence Peterson had died in 1988. *Son of a bitch, someone stole his identity.*

Looking out at the panoramic view she'd adored that morning, it now seemed like a two-dimensional watercolor painting. A mystery was forming, and she was in its midst; Maddy knew the feeling well.

The afternoon passed, and she was unsure how far to pursue things, but she decided to call Hannah Bates.

"FBI Albany field office," a woman answered.

"I'd like to speak with Agent Bates, please." Hannah had been with the New York State Police and led the investigation into The Glades. She also used to be Adam's supervisor. Back then, she was the highest-ranking African American woman among the state troopers and helped bring down Avery Jordan. As the first woman detective with the Oneida County Sheriff's Department, Maddy felt an affinity for the woman who had since taken a position with the FBI. She knew what it was like to be the odd person in a large organization.

"Special Agent Bates is unavailable now, but if you leave your name and number, I'll have her call you." She gave her the information.

Uneasiness grew in her gut, realizing her three-year hiatus from the world had ended. The sun had descended behind the mountains, and its glow painted the sky pink. "I feel like I'm back three years," she whispered, shaking her head with her arms crossed.

CHAPTER 4

Maddy hadn't touched her weapons in two years but pulled out the gun case and laid it on the kitchen table the following day. By opening the metal box, she was opening the door to her past. For most of her adult life, there was never a time she was without a weapon. As she disassembled the two Glocks, her thoughts drifted to the ceremony at The Glades, where she'd be later that day. It would be the first time she stepped foot in that place of many horrors since the night of the great fire three years earlier.

She worked on her weaponry, occasionally looking out the window at the mist and the sun trying to burn it off. She gazed across the lake but could not see The Glades mountain. The smell of gun oil brought back memories of learning to shoot as a teenager.

The years after her father's murder left her anxiety-ridden, and with her mother already deceased, she moved to Utica and lived with her grandmother. She feared the man who killed her father would kill her as well. Tormented as a young teen, she could not sleep alone and would run to her grandma's bed almost every night. Intuitively, she had known learning to shoot was the answer to her problem. She'd convinced her grandmother to let her take shooting lessons and work at becoming an expert with a handgun.

I can't believe I feel the need to do this again, she thought as she worked at readying the Glocks for use. She supposed it would always be that way for her. *It's who I am. I wish it could have been different, but it's just the way it is.*

The phone rang. She wiped the oil from her hands and answered. Rose was on the other end and asked Maddy if she was still considering attending the dedication ceremony. "Yes, I'd like to go."

"I have to work until noon. But I can go home, clean up and meet you back at Lena's at one thirty. Would that work for you?" Maddy said it would be fine. When they hung up, she looked at the parts and pieces scattered on the table and wasn't up for completing the project. She left things where they lay, poured a cup of not-quite-cold coffee, went out to the deck, and sat.

A slight breeze chilled her bare feet, and she wrapped her arms around herself to keep warm. The coolness awakened her mind, and smelling dying leaves reminded her how much she loved the mountains in the fall. Wondering where Adam was right then, she thought of lying next to him days earlier. *What kind of danger is he in?* An aching hollowness grew in her gut as she grew mindful of how circumstances could take away the people she loved.

She moved inside and into the shower, and instead of eating leftovers, she headed to Lena's restaurant with plenty of time for lunch before meeting Rose. Lena's was the only diner in town, and she'd become one of its regulars.

Maddy thought of the townspeople as she drove to the village. She knew she differed from them, but she always felt accepted. Maybe, she thought, it was because she'd stuck it out in Berry Lake for so long, with its forever winters and endless isolation. Life in the mountains was difficult in winter, and it might disagree with most city people. Yet deep down, she knew the real reason was she'd gone toe-to-toe with the wickedness at The Glades and came out victorious.

The mountain retreat had been like cancer, sucking the life out of the town through intimidation, corruption, and immorality. It had taken several lives among the villagers, including the beloved Doc Abrams, the

Black man who had healed their bodies, minds, and broken spirits. It was an unforgivable sin, and when Maddy killed the dreaded Sedgwick Neri, The Glades's enforcer, a silent cheer rose among them. The people of the Adirondack town were not sophisticated, but Maddy had had enough of refined people. They were authentic, and that was good enough for her.

She pulled up in front of Lena's and found a spot at the counter. After ordering a BLT and Coke, she noticed a Black man sitting a few stools down, staring at her. She did a double take, thinking it looked like Doc, but she realized it had to be his son, Jason.

"You must be Maddy Reynolds."

"And you must be Doc's son." He moved over two seats to sit next to her and shook her hand.

"My dad talked about you often."

She was the last person to see his father alive. She and Doc had met in the rain at the end of a muddy road one night, and he told her all he knew about Avery Jordan. His fear of being seen by The Glades's ever-present eyes proved accurate. The meeting cost him his life. They forced his car off a cliff on the way home and killed him.

"I thought a lot of your dad. This town lost a patron saint when it lost him."

"I'd like to discuss what happened to my father leading up to his death at some point."

Maddy understood how not knowing the details surrounding the death of a loved one felt. It was twenty years before she knew what had happened to her father on the night of his murder. She told him she'd be glad to talk about it anytime.

"Are you planning on attending The Glades Memorial dedication today?" he asked.

"Yes, but it seems strange to have a memorial dedicated to a place that brought so much pain and suffering to so many people."

Jason said that was why they have war memorials. "So people will never forget." She looked at the young man and realized he had his father's wisdom.

"So, what do you plan on doing with your dad's place?" The property had served as Doc's home and medical practice office for over thirty years, and she thought of him every time she drove past.

"It's funny that you ask. It's been sitting there all these years, and I haven't had the heart to sell it. Whenever I send a check to Ernie Pendergast, the guy who maintains it for us, I keep saying I need to decide what to do. My wife and I came to put it on the market this summer, but when we arrived, we fell in love with the area. We've decided starting a family in Berry Lake is what we want."

Jason said he'd been practicing in Pittsburgh since he finished his residency, but they wanted to end up in a small town. "This is as good a place as any. I'll be following in my father's footsteps."

It was the best news Maddy had heard in a long time. Doc Abrams had been the only physician in the area, and since his death, the locals had to travel a dozen miles to the health clinic in Star Lake when they needed care. People of poorer means didn't make the trip and instead paid the price with maladies fostered by neglect.

As Jason left the restaurant, Rose walked in. "I have butterflies in my stomach. My mind was on that summer three years ago all morning." Maddy didn't say it, but hers was too. They walked outside into the sunlight and got into Maddy's Jeep. Although it had been years since she had ascended the steep hill where The Glades once stood, it felt like yesterday. Thoughts of her last ride through the tall white pine forest flooded her head.

Near the top of the mountain, the taller trees were missing, destroyed by the fire. Young saplings grew in their place. When the women reached the top, a large granite stone stood alone instead of the sprawling log structures that had comprised The Glades.

Cars arrived and began filling the new stone parking area. They found a spot and walked to a vast lawn. Grass danced in the breeze, and a shiny stone at the center of the field looked like a colossal gravestone, making the scene feel holy.

She walked to the monument and read the inscription. *Here stood The Glades, a place dedicated to destroying all good in the human spirit. Let this monument forever serve as a reminder that God's grace will always prevail.*

Her mind flashed to the boy who started the fire that leveled the ancient edifice. *Oh, Hector,* she thought with her eyes flushed with tears. *I hope you've found peace wherever you are.* He had a short, tumultuous life filled with pain. The Glades had taken the lives of his sister and the man who was his only real father, Doc Abrams.

At fifteen, Hector stood undeterred against Avery Jordan when he realized the man was exploiting his sister and addicted her to heroin. Yet, his defiance made him a target, and the wicked place killed him. She had seen boys like him on the streets of Utica while in law enforcement, kids who vented their rage onto the world. They might become exceptional people if they could catch a break, but if not, they'd end up dead.

Avery Jordan's mistress, Naomi White, shot Hector in the back as he ran from Jordan's office that night. Memories poured into Maddy's head. The smell of smoke lingered, just as it had the night she and Adam entered a wall of flames, trying to locate the wounded young maverick. It was still as pungent as it was that night. When they found the boy, he lay dead on a sofa in Doc's abandoned house.

It was all too real; she hadn't expected to be transported back in time. She wasn't prepared for the emotional shock. Rose noticed her face contorting, went to her, took her by the arm, and led her to a chair. People took their seats as Maddy gazed into her hands, reliving the night of woe. Voices simmered, and soon, the only sound was the constant breeze traveling through the ancient hills.

A young reverend stepped up to the podium; like a song, his melodic voice carried a purposeful message. "It is central to the human character to seek meaning in our experience. From the littlest things known only to ourselves to grand historical events known to all humanity, we crave to know why."

"Some experiences, however, are too mysterious, elusive, or dark to grasp. They test the limits of understanding and make us doubt any good will come of them. What took place on this mountain is one. Yet, here we are, three years later, trying, seeking, and grappling to find its purpose. We are not here to glorify or judge, not even to mourn, but to shine a light on what happened and ever remember the capacity of human beings to fall into their own darkness."

The reverend concluded, "The evil done here touched many, and some are sitting among us. Others sold into sex slavery may still live in bondage. Let us take a moment to pray for all who have been so afflicted."

The ceremony ended, and everyone stood. Funeral-like heaviness and a soft mumbling hung over the crowd. Maddy noticed a woman standing alone, dressed in black. It was Abigail Hicks. Neri, the throat-cutter, had murdered her daughter after Avery Jordan used the girl and disregarded her like yesterday's newspaper. Maddy walked up and said hello, and the woman nodded.

"How are you, Abigail?"

"I'm okay, and you?"

"I'm okay." She gave her a sympathetic smile. Abigail had helped her by giving her a torn-up letter her daughter had written to Avery Jordan before they found her in the woods with her head almost cut off. Maddy had pieced the letter together and deciphered a large part of The Glades's mystery. The sad woman turned, and she watched her walk away.

Lester Best, the hardware store owner, stood nearby, waiting. "Hey, Maddy." He held his brimmed hat with both hands. "You haven't been by the store in a while; how are things?" She said things were fine, thinking of Rose's story about Lester and the black bear, trying not to laugh about losing control of himself. "I've got seasoned cherry wood coming in; let me know if you want a few cords, and I'll hold them for you."

She thanked him, said she'd let him know, and added that she was sorry to hear about his dog. "Thanks. Old Luke would have been fifteen next week." She patted his arm, and he nodded, acknowledging her kind thoughts.

Rose gave her a look that asked whether she wanted to stay or leave. Maddy tilted her head toward the parking area, and they walked to the Jeep. As they drove off, Rose said the event brought back many memories. "It's hard to believe all that happened."

It was late afternoon after dropping Rose at Lena's. The house was cold when she returned home. She got comfortable, built a fire, and opened a bottle of wine. She noticed the message light blinking. It was the girl with an Asian accent. "Hello, Ms. Reynolds. I'm sorry I hung up on you, but you need to help me. I'm afraid for my life. I'll try calling nine o'clock tomorrow morning."

Jesus, what can this be about? Maddy's stomach tightened; she crossed her arms and began pacing around until she calmed herself. She remembered the same sensation three years earlier as The Glades's tornado waited to pull her into its vortex.

While she and Adam had lived in their sanctuary, guarded by ancient mountains, she could pretend the world's woes were gone forever. But when she accepted the invitation to speak at the conference, it was like stepping on a raft, floating into misty waters. Now she was in an unknown place, shrouded in fog. Gerald Ellis, the redheaded guy, and the girl on the phone held pieces to a new puzzle to be solved and drama yet to unfold.

The fire burned, and she drifted further into herself, visiting old wounds – some that had healed, others that were still raw. She called to mind those she'd loved. Their faces flickered in the light as though they were with her.

She remembered Hector sitting in the very room with tears in his eyes, fearing he was losing his sister to The Glades. Then, the night she and her friend Jodi watched embers glow, reeling after their confrontation with Avery Jordan and Naomi White at the mountain retreat's gala event. Just a few weeks earlier, she and Adam had made love before the fire, and her longing for him grew.

The hour grew late, and the heaviness of the wine drove Maddy deeper, searching for her purpose. The reverend's words from the dedication came back to her. *We crave to know the reasons. Yet some experiences are too mysterious, elusive, or dark to grasp. They test the limits of understanding and make us doubt any good will come of them.* She supposed that was the case with her. Her battles against Cupid, and The Glades, had a purpose beyond her understanding. "I have to believe in that," she whispered to herself.

She lay on the sofa listening to the sounds of the dying fire, closed her eyes, and fell asleep. It was just after eight o'clock when she woke up the next day. She expected the girl to call at nine, so she made coffee and wondered what she might find out when they spoke. But by ten o'clock, the phone hadn't rung, and she knew the call would not come. Frustrated, she dropped onto the living room sofa, stared at the ceiling, and thought of Adam. "Be near me, babe," she whispered, pretending he was lying beside her.

CHAPTER 5

After two weeks without a word from Adam, Maddy withdrew further into herself. It was Monday, and cold November winds had blown low-hanging gray clouds over Berry Lake, forcing her to think of winter. She dressed in warm clothes and started for the hardware store to take care of things she'd typically do a month earlier.

A sudden biting wind whipped across her face when she stepped out of the Jeep in front of Lester's. Her eyes watered, and she remembered the lousy part of winter in the mountains. She stepped around a display of snow shovels and snowblowers crowding the entranceway, and although she had already made plans to have her road plowed, she grabbed a wooden-handled shovel to clear off the front steps and carried it to the counter. Lester stood wearing spectacles, examining an invoice.

"Why, Maddy, you're a sight for sore eyes." He looked at her over his glasses.

"Hi, Lester. Do you still have cherry firewood available?"

"Yup, I knew you'd need it, so I saved your usual ten cords. I can have Stick Larson drop it off by the end of the week if you'd like." She asked how much. "Thirty-five a cord delivered." She nodded and pulled out cash.

"You don't have to pay all at once if you don't want to."

"I may as well take care of it while I have the money." She handed over the three hundred and fifty for the cords and another ten for the shovel. Shoving the rest back into her jacket, she asked if he'd heard anything more about that black bear.

"Julie Barnes was here yesterday and said she'd had a run-in with him. He broke into her root cellar and tore it all to hell. He's an ornery one, alright. I'd be careful up there on your mountain. If he doesn't hibernate, and he's just the type that won't, there will be hell to pay around here this winter."

A mighty gust of wind rattled the picture windows at the front of the store, and the chimes over the door sounded out a tinkling alarm. They turned as leaves blew through the town, mixing with snow and pattering the glass. "Yep, I think it's gonna be a bad winter this year," Lester said. "We ain't had one in a while, and we're due."

When she left the hardware store, Maddy drove down the street to Lena's for lunch. It was close to noon, and the place looked packed. Rose waved her to an open spot at the counter. "I'll be right back to take your order."

"Are you Maddy Reynolds?" a woman with dirty blonde hair sitting at a booth behind her asked.

"Yes, are you new to the area?"

The woman said her name was Miranda Southworth, and she had just moved to Berry Lake from Elmira. "I started working as a nurse for Doctor Abrams, and he told me all about you."

"I didn't realize Jason opened his doors already. I'll have to stop by and say hello."

Rose returned to take Maddy's order. "I see you've met Jason Abrams's new nurse."

"Yes, and I'm glad to see we'll have a medical practice in town again." After Maddy had ordered, Rose started walking away, but Miranda asked her to bring cream for her coffee when she returned. The woman got her coffee from the booth and sat next to Maddy.

"So, what brings you to the area?" Maddy asked.

"I recently went through a divorce. I needed a complete change of scenery and wanted to live close to nature. When I saw Doctor Abrams's advertisement for a nurse in Berry Lake, I jumped on it."

"I went through a divorce years ago," Maddy said. "My daughter was six, and thank God my grandmother was alive to help. I don't know how I would have managed without her. Do you have children?"

"Thank goodness, no. Right now, my biggest concern is getting bored in this new place during the winter months." Maddy remembered having the same concern when she first came to Berry Lake. "Maybe we can meet at my place for lunch sometime when you're settled."

"I'd like that. Thank you." As she stood to leave, Rose came over and placed Maddy's food on the counter.

"Miranda seemed very lovely. Let's have lunch with her at my place soon."

"Sure, but let's do it on a clear day so we can impress her with that awesome view from your kitchen. Oh, boy, I've been itching to make an apple pie."

When she finished and was heading back to her place, she thought about Miranda and how unusual it was for a woman to move to a secluded place like Berry Lake alone. It's what Maddy had done when she left her detective job after being wounded in a shoot-out with the Donnolly gang. When fate gave her an exit ticket, she took it. She didn't know Miranda's entire story but thought she must be brave; she respected that in a person.

When she returned home, her daughter was on her mind. Amber was struggling with her new job the last time they had spoken. She called, and it was a relief to hear her sounding excited. The two were close, and Maddy always kept Amber a priority in her life. But she had worried how her daughter would cope when she took a job three thousand miles away without her mother nearby.

"Hi, honey, it's Mom," she said when Amber answered.

"Oh, Mom, I'm so glad you called."

"You sound so excited; tell me what's going on. The last time we talked, deadlines at the publishing house had you stressed."

"I got through all that, but last night, something incredible happened. You will not believe it, Mom. Todd gave me a ring. We're engaged!" She shrieked with excitement. "I'm getting married. Isn't that unbelievable?"

Maddy didn't know what to say. She'd met Todd twice, and he seemed nice enough, but to jump into marriage after knowing him only eight months seemed like a giant leap. She remembered feeling that way when she and Jack married. *Look how shitty it turned out for me. But I will not rain on her parade.*

"You're right; it's unbelievable. Have you set a date?"

"We want to be married in April, maybe the twenty-sixth. I'm so excited; I can't stand still." After she caught her breath, Amber added, "You'll have to come to San Diego and help me with all the arrangements."

Maddy did her best not to show her concern for what she thought was an impulsive decision. As Amber rambled through lists of tasks that needed to be done and decisions that had to be made, Maddy realized she had not met Todd's parents, nor could she remember where he was from. She tried to back her way out of the embarrassing lack of attention she'd paid to her daughter's fiancé when they met by asking how Todd's parents felt about the news.

Amber hesitated, stammered, and said, "They're not too keen on it." Taken aback, Maddy asked her to explain. "I'm not sure why. They just want us to take more time."

She sensed more was going on than Amber was letting on, so she dug deeper. "Honey, I don't remember where Todd and his family are from. Please remind me."

"You don't know, because I never told you." That got her mother's attention. She waited and had to ask her what was going on.

"They live in Los Altos Hills. It's an affluent area near San Francisco."

Maddy felt like she'd been kicked in the gut. She was unprepared for Amber's intimidation by her fiancé's family's status. "His father is a dean at Stanford University, his mother is an engineering professor, and they are wealthy."

"What about their wealth made you not tell me?"

"I was afraid it would make you feel uncomfortable."

"How about you? Does it make you feel uncomfortable?"

"Yes," Amber said as she wept. For the first time, Maddy glimpsed how her daughter saw herself through the lens of status. Unprepared, her heart sank at the thought that Todd's parents might think Amber wasn't good enough for their son. She collected her thoughts and asked if they had said something to make her feel that way.

"No, they're nice to me. But I can't believe how anxious I feel when I'm with them."

"How about Todd? Does he know how you feel?"

"He doesn't understand why I feel this way. How could he? I don't even understand myself." She huffed as she wept. "I mean, at Cornell, I met a lot of rich kids, and I became friends with some. But I feel intimidated about being part of a wealthy family. I'm afraid I won't meet their expectations."

"You'll be marrying Todd, not his parents. Do you feel Todd has unrealistic expectations of you?"

"No."

"Then it sounds like this is coming from within you."

"I suppose. Since I moved to San Diego, I feel much more conscious of status than I used to. Things are very different here than in Utica."

She knew there was little she could do to assuage her daughter's discomfort other than to give her support. "Honey, you listed everything you need to do to be married in the spring a moment ago. There is nothing wrong with that, but discussing your feelings with Todd might be more important."

After a long silence, Amber said, "You're right, Mom. I've been putting the cart before the horse. Before I rush into this, I need to understand my feelings and why I'm so uncomfortable with Todd's family. I guess I have to remember what Great Grandma always said, 'Remember who you are; don't be more and don't let anyone make you feel less.' I didn't know how much this was bothering me until now."

"That's why it's good to get things off your chest." When they hung up, Maddy started thinking about when she and Jack were in love. Although she was pregnant when they married, she didn't feel forced. She believed they were a perfect match. *But the job, a kid, and money pressure led him to the bottle, and things went downhill.*

She tried to support him through the hard times, but when she found out he was shacking up with a young blonde from the office, the betrayal was too much to bear. It tore her apart, and she insisted on a divorce.

She wished she had listened to her grandmother, who knew Jack would not make her happy from the start. Her grandma told her that even though she was pregnant, she still had a right to happiness and Jack could give it to her. It pained her to think that her daughter might have to go through an unhappy marriage, but she felt it was one more thing she couldn't control in her life.

Two gloomy days had passed, and it was late morning. The sound of a puttering engine brought Maddy to the back door, and she saw Stick Larson driving a tractor, pulling a load of firewood. She went to the deck and waved at him to stop. "Do you mind putting it near the basement doors?"

"Sure, would you like me to stack it for ya?"

"Please do, and I'll pay you." As he started pulling around, the phone rang. It was Hannah Bates.

"It's been a while; how are things on your mountain?" Hannah asked with a chuckle. She had been to her place a few times and always seemed amused that the famous detective would choose to live in the wilderness.

"Winter's coming, and it's getting cold. I'm calling to see if my credit is still good. I need a favor."

"It depends on what it is."

"I have a phone number, and I need the address of its location."

"Your credit might cover that. Do I even want to know why you want this address? On second thought, never mind. I don't think I want to know. Give me the number, and I'll see what I can do, but no promises."

When she gave her the number, Hannah said, "Oh, all the way down to Virginia. Now I *know* I don't want to know what it's about. I'll get back to you."

Not knowing where the information would lead, Maddy felt she had no choice but to locate the girl who feared for her life. That's how it was with her; when it got right down to it, she'd always say 'fuck it, I'm going to do what I think is right.' It was a quality she once berated herself for having, especially after suffering wounds from ferocious encounters. In time, however, she accepted it was an indelible aspect of her nature.

With the sound of clunking wood, she headed out to help Stick. He was almost finished when she walked around to the side of the house. "I can't believe you stacked so much wood in such a short time." She picked up a few pieces and handed them to him.

"It's not so hard once you get into a rhythm." She helped with the last of it and asked how much for stacking.

"Oh, I don't know."

"Is twenty-five okay?"

"That's too much, Maddy."

She handed him a twenty and a five. "I think it's about right." He thanked her and asked if she'd heard about the giant black bear that had been raising hell around Berry Lake.

"Yes, I heard about what happened to Lester."

"Do you keep your trash in the basement on the other side of those doors?" He pointed to the walkout basement.

"Yes, why do you ask?"

"Well, I don't mean to be the one to say it, but those doors won't keep that guy out."

"Really?" She gazed at the solid wooden doors with her hands on her hips, thinking the damn beast must be mighty powerful. "What do you suggest?"

"Well, double-bag leftover food and keep it in airtight bins. Try to empty them often. The more in there, the easier it will be to pick up the scent."

The sky became dark when Stick got on the tractor and puttered away. A hollowness grew in her stomach, and she wondered where Adam was. He felt far away. Snow started falling; a muffled silence covered the lonely hills, and Maddy carried her sadness inside.

CHAPTER 6

Naomi White

Naomi stood on the veranda of her expensive Manhattan apartment, gazing down at chic boutique shops and gourmet restaurants thirty floors below. It was a warm November morning. A light shawl covered the woman's sensitive albino skin, protecting it from the sun as she reminisced about how far she'd come in wealth and status. *I've played my cards right, and it's paid off.*

Naomi loved the busyness of people visiting her swanky neighborhood on Saturday mornings, as long as it remained on the street below – she didn't like people. *I've come a long way since New Orleans. It's hard to believe it's been over twenty years since I sold my brothel and joined Avery at The Glades. A lot of water has gone under the bridge.*

The closest Naomi had ever come to loving someone was Avery Jordan. Devilishly handsome, intelligent, and sophisticated, he respected her abilities and gave her the adulation she craved. But what she loved most about him was how easily she could play his insecure self, like a violin, to get what she wanted.

She thought the poor man took himself far too seriously. She reflected on how he blew his brains out as he burned in The Glades fire. *But he was just a means to an end when it got right down to it. I'd still be stuck in foul New Orleans if it weren't for him.*

She had learned from her mother, who was also a child of New Orleans's red-light district, that the minds of most men did not rest between their ears, but rather hung between their legs. This simple understanding never failed. Using her beauty and sexuality, she could open all doors to men, including their wallets. She wanted everything Avery Jordan had, and that's what she got.

The smells of delicious foods, the sounds of people laughing, and the constant electricity in the New York City air filled her with self-satisfaction. *It's a glorious day.*

Although Jordan was brilliant, his weakness for Naomi's allure was powerful, allowing the vixen's name to find its way onto titles of The Glades's liquid assets. Many months after the place evaporated in the fire, she added a substantial sum to her already bountiful trove of treasure. As she basked in the glorious day, the phone rang, disrupting her reverie. *I suppose I should answer that.*

She went inside, picked up, and heard a deep, gravelly voice. "Have you watched the news today?"

"Who in the hell is this?" she barked.

"How quickly we forget." Like a sledgehammer pounding a memory into her consciousness, she remembered the voice belonged to The Guy. An icy shudder shook her.

"No, I have not." At first, she was unsure what to do, then realized something was on the TV he wanted her to see. She walked to the entertainment room and picked up the remote.

"Turn on CNN, Miss White." She flipped to the channel as a newswoman interviewed a congressman. The subscript at the bottom of the screen said, *Congressman Suarez calls for an investigation into sex trafficking.*

"Are you watching, Miss White?"

"Yes, I'm watching."

"Good," he said with disdain. "We understand Avery Jordan kept records of all visitors to The Glades and their purchases. Are we correct?"

"Yes, he referred to it as the ledger."

"Do you know where the ledger is?" Naomi hesitated, then said she believed the fire had destroyed it. "The ledger had a polished tungsten crest on its cover, correct?"

"Yes, that's correct."

"Tungsten melts at six thousand degrees, Miss White. The temperatures of the fire at The Glades would not have exceeded two thousand degrees." *Where is he going with this?*

"Our people on the inside inspected every morsel of evidence collected from the inferno. They found no crest. Do you know what that means?"

"I think so."

"It means, Miss White, the ledger still exists. And do you know what else it means?"

"No."

"It also means many prominent friends will go to prison if the wrong people find it." After a few seconds of silence, The Guy shouted, "Find the fucking ledger!" and hung up.

Her mind went blank, a rare occurrence for her. She went to an end table where she kept cigarettes for emergencies, opened its drawer, selected a Nat Sherman Black and Gold, and lit up. She sat on the sofa, her cigarette jittering, trying to calm herself, thinking of how to approach what seemed to be an impossible task.

Calm down, Naomi. You've been in jams before and always figured things out. Now, where was the ledger last seen? She remembered it lay on Avery Jordan's desk an hour before the fire. *Yes, I remember he reviewed the sex auction numbers and shouted, "We did it!"*

Avery was like a kid who'd won a free trip to Disneyland when he realized he'd generated enough money to pay the final note on The Glades to The Guy. He'd brooded for weeks, fearing what would happen if he couldn't fulfill the obligation.

He let no one touch his precious ledger and almost always placed it inside his wall safe before leaving his office. Naomi wondered if, in his excitement, he deviated from his obsessive pattern. *Because it wasn't in the evidence gathered by the police, it could not have made it into the safe.*

Someone must have taken it from the desk and out of the building. But who?

Wait, she thought. *Hector Lemont had something under his arm when he jumped from Avery's office window.* Her mind returned to the moment the kid was about to jump. *It was a paper bag. That little shit must have taken the ledger and put it in the bag.*

Maddy Reynolds had found Hector dead in a house in Berry Lake. *But it doesn't make sense that Reynolds found the ledger. If she had, she would have turned it into the authorities, and the public lynchings that The Guy fears would have already taken place. No way Reynolds found the ledger,* she concluded.

She realized its whereabouts might have gone unnoticed forever if it weren't for the congressional probe. The media coverage now put it front and center in the minds of dangerous people. *Once its existence becomes known, law enforcement, politicians, and every swinging dick who has visited the place will have an interest in finding it. If it falls into the wrong hands, they'll kill me.*

She knew what The Guy would do if she failed to find the damn thing. He was a mafioso. Jordan had cringed every time he called. Avery told Naomi how his father cut a deal with the mob to lend him the money to establish The Glades. It needed to be paid within ten years. *If I don't pay it back by September, nineteen eighty-four, they will kill me,* he'd always reminded her.

She paraded around her flat and lit another smoke; her mind was stuck on the night of the fire. She remembered the loan had been due the following day. Avery had made it out of the building as the place burned. He had watched the conflagration from outside, but suddenly realized the ledger containing the bank codes was in his office. The codes were the only means to transfer the money from auction attendees to Avery's bank account. Without them, he could not pay The Guy, and he'd be a dead man.

Naomi was not with him as he watched the fire, and although she was told he had asked everyone where she was, she'd already exited the tragedy. *I'm sorry, honey,* she thought. *When I had a chance to get out, I took it.* As the fire raged, she and Darius Girard had flown out on a private plane from The Glades airfield.

The notion of a frightened Avery seeking her out before running to his painful death penetrated Naomi's icy heart. She felt a pang of sadness. *He always came to me when he was afraid. I knew how to soothe the frightened little boy within him. I could have talked sense into him.*

She wondered what it must have been like when he reached his burning office and found the ledger and the codes gone. *Poor Avery.* She was told security guards outside tried to save him. They heard him screaming until a gunshot ended his agonizing squeals. Despite his burned body, everyone believed he would've rather eaten a bullet than face The Guy. Avery Jordan's sad story ended well for her. *Until now,* she thought. Six cigarettes and many memories later, Naomi went to her desk, pulled out an address book, and began looking up phone numbers of people to engage in the search.

She could not believe how rattled she felt. Her fingers trembled, and her neck was tight as a wound-up rubber band; she felt like she might snap. The gravity of her situation started sinking in, and the booze in the next room crossed her mind, but she nixed the idea. *That's the last thing I need now; I must keep my wits.*

The thought of running tempted her, but she decided it was a non-starter. She once knew someone who tried running from the mob. They found the man with his hands and feet in his coat pockets and dick in his mouth. No, running was not an option. She thought her best bet was to narrow down the likely places the ledger might be, and Darius Girard was the place to start.

Like her, Darius worked with Avery Jordan. As his personal assistant, screening calls, he kept his schedule and monitored his whereabouts. Naomi didn't have a lot of respect for the man because he wasn't street-smart like her, but he was book-smart, which drew Avery to him. She tracked down his phone number and called.

"Hello, Darius, it's Naomi; remember me?" After a long silence, he said he did. "It wasn't easy finding you down there in San Antonio. Were you trying to hide from me?" She laughed, enjoying busting on the fragile man.

"What do you want, Naomi?"

"I want to talk with you about the good old days at The Glades."

"I'm not part of that world anymore. I have a new life here. My family and business are important to me; everything's legitimate."

"Oh, but Darius, it's not so easy to run from what you've done."

"What *I've* done? You mean what *you've* done." Naomi snickered. She never considered him a powerful man; indeed, not of the caliber of Sedgwick Neri, the throat-cutter. But his intelligence set him apart, and she knew she had to be careful.

"Well, that's neither here nor there. I'm calling because I'm paying you a visit tomorrow, so don't try running. I know all about your pretty young wife, the two boys, and that ostentatious restaurant on the River Walk. You know me; I have eyes everywhere."

"What's this about, Naomi?"

"If I could discuss it on the phone, I wouldn't be flying eighteen hundred miles now, would I?" Darius was silent. "I will meet you tomorrow at your restaurant at about three in the afternoon. *Girard's,* I believe the name is. Bye-bye!"

When she hung up, she took her cigarette to the veranda and gazed down at the city. But everything had changed. *Two hours ago, I was getting off on how I had it made; now, I wonder if I'll be alive in a month. Where can the fucking ledger be? It's going to be like finding a needle in a haystack.*

She lit another cigarette, went to the liquor cabinet, tossed ice cubes in a glass, and filled it with bourbon. The sting felt good going down, numbing nerve endings, dulling the brain. The doorbell rang; she looked at her watch and remembered. *It's Drake. Shit, I forgot.*

The dashing young dark-skinned man walked inside, looking like he had just stepped out of GQ magazine. He stood with a bouquet of arranged flowers, dressed in a suit, shirt opened, and smelling good enough to eat. "Oh, Drake, I forgot. Please come in."

Still in his twenties, the young stud approached and held her. For a moment, she melted, wishing she could steal the boy away to her bed. She thought it wasn't fair, so she stopped him from kissing her neck. "No, sweetie, something's come up that's gotten poor Naomi all tense. I don't think I'd be much fun tonight. I'll give you your money."

Drake stroked her cheek and said, "Maybe I can relieve that tension for you." He put his mouth close and bit her ear. Naomi's head fell back, letting him kiss around her neck, and she moaned.

"Oh, dear boy, you do not know what you do to me." She felt her blood rising. "But I have to leave town early tomorrow, so please stop. We'll be naughty another time soon, I promise. Let me get your money." She grabbed an envelope as she nuzzled him to the door, and when he left, she thought, *What a crime.*

Drake was one of a few select young men Naomi paid for sex. It was a perfect arrangement, she thought. *He makes enough to pay tuition at Columbia, and I meet my sensual needs.*

After she made plane reservations and packed a bag, she refreshed her drink and took it to the balcony. The sun had gone down, nightclubs were lit up like Paris in an impressionistic painting, and the night was alive. Music with a beat, mixed with laughter, filled the street with weekend mirth. Yet, for the first time in her life, Naomi felt her best years were over. *So much has passed.*

All of her life, she'd been able to put a smiley face on the damage she left behind and the people she'd hurt. Her destructive behavior had always slid off her as if she were Teflon. Proud of her self-sufficiency, she had kept love away, using physical-only relationships to hold people at a distance. But at that moment, she felt alone. Overwhelmed, she shuddered, thinking she'd lived without the love of others, and wondered what it would be like facing death without someone. She finished her drink, closed her mind, and went to bed.

It was 12:46 the next afternoon, and her flight landed in San Antonio. She caught a cab to the Hotel Valencia on the Riverwalk and checked in by 2:30. After changing, she walked along the winding San Antonio River with its outdoor cafés. People sat drinking margaritas and snacking on Tex-Mex hors d'oeuvres as she looked for Darius's restaurant.

Nestled in a bend, *Girard's* stood alone along the path. When she walked inside, a lanky, bald, and dark-skinned Darius Girard sat at a table with his arms folded as though he was waiting for her. She walked up and let her sweeter side show.

"Hello, Darius; you've done well for yourself." He gave her a half-smile, gestured to a chair across from him, and she sat down. A server appeared, and she ordered ice water.

"On the wagon, Naomi?" he asked, with a sneer breaking through his worried expression.

"No. We have an important issue to discuss, and I in no way want to misrepresent its deadly significance." She waved a napkin before her face and added, "I forgot how damn hot it is down here."

Darius remained silent until she got her water, then said, "So what is so critical you had to track me down?"

"The Guy has reemerged. You remember The Guy, don't you?"

The color from Darius's face drained. He held his stomach like he was about to belch and started tapping his fingers on the table. She knew he remembered because he would take The Guy's calls and send them through to Jordan, who always dreaded the man with the gravelly voice.

"I'm afraid he's not happy, Darius."

Girard eked out, "What does he want?" He looked as if he'd been coldcocked.

"He wants Avery's ledger."

"Why the fuck does he want that? All that's history; it's been three years."

"There's a congressional investigation underway into sex trafficking, and as you know, there are some very important people on that list."

"The fire destroyed the ledger. Didn't you tell him?"

"I did, but he can prove that it didn't. And so, one reason I've come here is so you can help me save both of our lives." Darius sighed and looked at the table, reflecting on what the news meant to his new life.

After simmering for a moment, he blurted out, "How the hell am I supposed to know what happened to the fucking thing? Jordan always kept it in his safe; that's all I know."

"It wasn't in the safe," she said. "I believe Hector Lemont had it before his accident."

"But he's dead!"

"I know that, but he didn't die right away. He made it to the village and died in an abandoned house. They didn't find it on him, so we need to figure out who else might know where it is. You had all the contacts with the locals; I couldn't stand the lowlifes. So think, Mr. Girard. Think real hard; who else might know something?"

He sat back, let his arms drop, and looked in another direction as though his mind was drifting. "The only people I dealt with in the town were the chief of police, who's now in prison because he was on our payroll, and Ernie Pendergast, from Pendergast Farms, where we bought all our fresh produce." Then, as an afterthought, he added, "Wait, there was that tall guy who made deliveries. His name was Larson; they called him Stick. We suspected he was giving Hector Lemont rides to The Glades in his truck."

She wrote the information on a notepad and said it was a place to start. "Now, for the other reason I came here." Darius gawked at her like he was waiting to be assaulted. "I don't need to tell you who The Guy represents and what they can do. So, if the FBI or anyone else comes here asking questions, tell them you handled the purchasing for The Glades and knew nothing about the trafficking part of the business. If I'm asked about your role, I'll back that up. If anyone asks what I did, tell them I handled public relations for the catering part of the business. That's what you must tell them."

Girard put his elbows on the table and rested his forehead on his hands like he was about to vomit. As he shook his head, she said, "Now, Darius, it's not as bad as that. All we need to do is keep our stories straight, and we'll be fine. When we figure out what happened to the ledger, I'll make sure we retrieve the damn thing."

She got up and left Darius sitting at the table in an emotional stupor. Nothing was left to say; the past had returned to haunt them.

As Naomi flew back to New York that night, she gazed at the black emptiness thirty thousand feet below. Part of her life was ending, and everything she worked to attain was about to end unless she found the ledger. To survive, she would need to use every trick she'd learned, from her New Orleans brothel days to her years of sex trafficking at The Glades. She wasn't about to give up without a fight. She would do anything to keep what she had, including kill.

CHAPTER 7

Maddy

The dreary skies that hung over the region cleared out. The sun shone, and the crisp November air lifted Maddy's spirits. It was an excellent day to visit Jason Abrams at his new office, and after showering, she dressed and headed for town.

It was just noon when she walked into an empty waiting room. She heard a voice say hello from another room. It was Miranda, and when Maddy walked in, she looked surprised and harried.

"Oh, hi. Jason is running errands during the lunch break." Behind her, bandages, gauze, tape, and bottles of liquids and pills lay strewn over a counter. Miranda gazed at the chaos and said she was just trying to organize supplies. "You know how physicians are; they're intelligent but not the neatest people in the world."

Maddy asked how she was adjusting to Berry Lake. When Miranda shrugged and said she was catching up on her reading, she assumed the woman wasn't enjoying her stay in the mountain community. She said she came by to figure out something Jason might need. "I'd like to get him an office warming gift. Any ideas?"

"What he needs, you can't give him," Miranda complained. "That fireplace needs to be fixed. It's damp, and I wear my coat most of the time. We tried starting a fire last week, but the smoke wouldn't go up the flue."

She wrapped her hands around herself as though trying to keep warm. "He has inherited a lot of mismatched coffee cups, and some have chips. A set of mugs might make an excellent gift."

"Perfect." Before leaving, she reminded her of the open invitation for lunch at her place. Miranda smiled and said she'd take her up on it soon. "I'm still getting my feet on the ground. Thursdays are best, though, because I only work half-days."

On the drive home, Maddy thought about the house she was just in. It was where she and Adam found Hector lying on Doc's sofa. The power company had turned the electricity off, and it was dark. Adam had flashed his light around, and Hector's lifeless arm hung as he stared with his eyes frozen open. The boy who had lost so much to The Glades had fallen to its wickedness.

She had leaned over, pushed his long blood-caked hair aside, and kissed his forehead, giving him the mother's love he needed. Lost in rumination, a white Volvo sitting in front of her house startled her back to the present. She reached for her weapon in the door panel, but it wasn't there. *Fuck!*

Keeping the Glock close by was a habit she'd let go of in recent years. She had felt safe in her reclusive life and had dropped the protective practice. She pulled next to the Volvo, but its smoke-tinted glass prevented her from seeing the driver. She got out of the Jeep, and his window lowered. A man in his late thirties, wearing reflective sunglasses, smiled.

"Maddy Reynolds?"

"That's me. Who are you?"

"Aaron Purdy. I'm an assistant to Congressman Herman Suarez." The guy stepped out of the car, stretched his back, and looked at the mountain across from hers. "It's pretty up here, but it's far. I didn't know how far it was." The tall, clean-shaven man held out his hand, and Maddy shook it with caution.

"I suppose you're gonna tell me what this is all about."

"Oh, I'm sorry. I'm just a little overwhelmed by all this. I grew up in Tampa; this area is amazing."

"You're lucky you came today. If you were here three days ago, you'd be standing in six inches of snow. It would have ruined your Bostonians."

The guy laughed, looked at her as if trying to size her up, and said he had something vital to discuss. "Can we go inside?" *There's that damn word again. Gerald Ellis said he had something 'vital' to discuss, too.*

"Well, come in, and you can explain what's so vital."

She told him to get comfortable in the living room while she put on a pot of coffee. He sat near the fireplace. From the kitchen, she asked if he always visited people unannounced. "Well, what I have to discuss is very important, and I figured if I had to, I'd camp out until you showed up."

Cocky son of a bitch, she thought to herself. She laughed and quipped that it might not have been a good idea because a rogue black bear had been terrorizing the area. "He might like to have you and your car for dinner."

Purdy half chuckled as if he wasn't sure she was kidding, then changed the subject. "This is an amazing place you have here." He looked up at the inlaid wood on the vaulted ceiling and the floor-to-ceiling fieldstone fireplace.

"Thanks, I like it too." She brought a tray and set it down on the table near him. When he fixed his coffee the way he wanted, she gave him a look that she hoped said, *Okay, you're here and have your coffee; now tell me what the hell is going on.*

He set the cup down and said, "Congressman Suarez is starting a congressional investigation into sex trafficking. The other day, it became public; you may have seen it on television."

She laughed and said the reception in the area wasn't good, and it was the first she had heard of it. "We see you as a crucial witness. We know all about your background, going back to Cupid. Your history, reputation in law enforcement, and what you experienced at The Glades make you credible."

"Before we go any further, I need to know what happened to Gerald Ellis."

Aaron looked into his lap. "We don't know for sure. He was coming to talk to you about what I am here to discuss."

"That was no simple hit and run," Maddy said. "It was intentional. Shiny black Cadillacs don't just run people down in broad daylight and disappear without a trace. What the hell's going on, Mr. Purdy?"

Purdy gazed at her with a smirk. "I was told you were different. That was an understatement." He crossed his arms. "We think someone murdered Ellis when word leaked out about the probe. Some powerful men participated in The Glades's activities and similar events around the country; several don't want their reputations ruined."

"Are you saying they're willing to kill to stop your investigation?"

"We think so."

"Do you have any idea who may have killed Ellis?"

Purdy looked to the side and said, "No."

Like hell you don't, she thought. She knew when a person didn't look you in the eye when answering direct questions, they were hiding something.

"I need to know everything you know, Mr. Purdy. Maybe I'm on their radar. I'm not fucking around; my life has been a litany of confrontations with people who've wanted to kill me. I fear my nine lives are running out."

Purdy looked at her astonished, as though he wasn't expecting such direct talk from a woman who appeared as mild as Maddy. "We think Gerald Ellis was onto something big. He worked independently, and we're not sure what he had. Someone threatened by his work likely killed him. Ms. Reynolds, one central question has been troubling us."

Maddy sat down, folded her arms, and hoped to get something substantial from the guy. "There must have been some documentation of The Glades's activity. You know, a means of accounting, like a logbook. We want to identify people who attended those events. With such a document, we can put many bad people behind bars. We're hoping you might help us."

"I witnessed a sex auction the night before the fire. About thirty men took part, and each flew home on a private plane with at least one woman he had purchased; some had two. It was a masquerade event, and their faces weren't visible. As far as an accounting book goes, I don't know of any such thing. So, Mr. Purdy, I can't help you."

She wanted the guy out of her house; he was invading her safe space, but he didn't seem to give up. Maddy was fighting a magnetic force, pulling her into something she didn't understand. Yet part of her felt she couldn't turn away. Confused by her ambivalence, she let the guy continue.

"How about people who worked at The Glades itself? Jordan and Neri are dead, but what about Naomi White and Darius Girard? Do you know anything about them?"

"Girard didn't seem to fit in with the rest. He wasn't as mean as they were. But Naomi ran the show, and she's nasty. She killed a fifteen-year-old boy that night; shot him in the back. I can't believe your people haven't tracked and prosecuted her by now."

"They tried, but they didn't have enough evidence. We heard she killed the Lemont boy, but the only eyewitness to the murder was Daniel Mosher, a deputy sheriff on Jordan's payroll, and he died the night of the fire."

She flashed back to the night. It was as if a lightning bolt had struck her. Mosher was about to put a bullet in the back of her head when Adam, undercover then, took him out. She realized Adam might be involved with the Suarez investigation and wanted to know more.

"Let me ask you something. Are the New York State Police supporting your probe?"

"Why do you ask?"

"Just answer my question, please." She looked into his eyes for a sign that he was telling the truth or lying. He blinked when he said he couldn't say. "You already did." Her heart sank into her stomach. *Adam's in the middle of it; I know it.* "So, what do you people hope to accomplish?"

"We want to raise public awareness about sex trafficking in America. Most people think it's only a problem in developing nations. If we can raise consciousness, we'll get the support we need to fight it in Congress. We also want to jail the people involved in this barbarism and free women still in bondage."

She knew as well as anyone about the horrors of the sexual exploitation of young women. She dealt with it with Cupid, who raped little girls before killing them, and at The Glades when Avery Jordan addicted women to heroin and then sold their services. She also knew that few people, other than those affected, cared. "You need to tell me more. This has been going on for a long time; why now? There's something you're not telling me."

He sat back in his chair with a quizzical stare. "Yes, there is more. What I'm going to tell you needs to remain confidential. Herman Suarez was born in Mexico and became a U.S. citizen when he was forty-five. While still in Mexico, Marianna, his daughter, was abducted and sold as a sex slave. She was thirteen." Aaron seemed to choke up. He composed himself and continued. "They found her dead in a hotel room in Tucson, Arizona. This is very personal for the congressman."

With that, Maddy let her guard down. "I understand. I have found that people, especially political types, talk a good game, but they disappear when the wind shifts. It doesn't sound like your congressman is one of these. I'll do what I can to help."

Maddy needed to hear the backstory to let the Suarez initiative into her world. Fast talkers who expounded high-minded reasons she should give her support had hurt her in the past. Now, people who expected her trust had to earn it.

A look of relief came over Aaron's face. He stood, appearing as though he had accomplished his purpose for visiting. As he was about to leave, he stopped, looked at her, and seemed unsure of what he wanted to say.

"There's something more I think I should share with you, Maddy – is it okay if I call you Maddy?" She nodded. "If we are right about there being a document with names of people who took part at The Glades, there'll be desperate men trying to find it." He hesitated as if there was more, but Maddy finished for him.

"And I will be a target."

"Yes, we think so. We understand you're an expert with a handgun. Is that true?"

"Yes."

"Perhaps you should stay armed."

"Thank you for the advice; I already am."

He looked at her, and as he walked through the kitchen to the back door, he gazed at the view and said, "I do like this place."

She walked him to his car, and he handed her his card before getting in. "We know you work alone, but please let us know if you find anything." She watched dust kicking up on the road as he left. When he was gone, she stood alone and realized there was no going back to the way it had been the last three years. *Those days are over.* As she walked back inside, she thought of Adam and wondered if they were in the same fight.

CHAPTER 8

Purdy's visit remained on Maddy's mind for several days. She thought of how naïve she had been. *I can't believe I thought the ugliness ended when the sex auctions stopped. How foolish I was. I should have known evil doesn't just go away. It lingers until it's destroyed.*

She was trying to come to terms with her place in the grand scheme of events, and it was hard to face that she'd been avoiding reality for three years. Although she was tucked away on her mountain, the enemy still lurked about.

It was night, and she opened a window, letting in the cool air. She looked into the darkness, listening to night sounds and marveling at how nature readied itself for winter. *I, too, must prepare for what's coming.* She wanted it all to be over after The Glades, the fighting, the bloodshed, the death. *But delusion lies between what we want and what is,* she thought. *Aaron Purdy shattered my denial.* Her mind wandered while trying to go about her business as usual over the following days. She wondered what the next surprise in the unfolding saga might be.

The weather was fine on Thursday, and she drove to Things Forgotten Antique and Gift Shop. Julie Barnes came out from a back room. "How lovely it is to see you. How can I help you, Maddy?"

"I'm looking for an office warming gift for Jason Abrams's new medical practice. He needs a new set of coffee mugs. I'd like them to be different, maybe antique. Julie scrunched her lips, thinking, then said she had something that might be perfect.

"Come, let me show you." She walked to a table where books lay open and pulled one close as Maddy looked on. She flipped the pages and stopped, ran her fingers down, and pointed to a picture of antique French handmade mugs.

"What do you think?"

"They're gorgeous, but they're expensive."

"I can give you a third off." Maddy thought, nodded, and asked how long it would take to get them. "Two weeks."

"I'll take them."

The woman filled out the order form, and Maddy noticed a photograph of what appeared to be a backyard on the counter. "My God, what happened?" She was looking at two heavy wooden doors torn off their hinges, lying on the ground with smashed fruits and vegetables, crushed wicker baskets, and destroyed garden tools in the photo.

"That's the damage that bear did to my root cellar. I'm sending this to the insurance company, hoping to get money to help with the repairs." *No wonder Lester lost his bowels. The thing must be ferocious.*

After she left a deposit with Julie, she headed back home, and as she drove, Purdy's words returned to her. *We want to free women still in bondage.* She wondered how many women sold the night of the masquerade auction still lived as sex slaves and how many had died. *Those girls do not have the luxury of denial. If they're alive, they live their suffering every day.*

It had become routine to check for a message from Adam whenever she entered her place. The light blinked when she walked in, but the voice belonged to Hannah Bates. "I have the address you asked for. It's 944 Bleeker Road, Arlington, Virginia. Good luck."

Now, what do I do? It was a moment of truth. Jumping into the girl's situation with both feet might lead to unforeseen troubles, yet turning away violated everything she believed in. After stewing for an hour, she picked up the phone and called Jodi Novak.

Jodi was a friend, but not just any friend. She had saved Maddy's life the night they were in the grip of Cupid. She was just fourteen at the time, and having grown up in Vietnam during the war, she was mature beyond her years. After digging out her new Denver phone number, Maddy called, and Jodi's voice was like a songbird on the other end of the line when she answered.

"Jodi, it's Maddy."

"Maddy! It's so good to hear your voice."

"It's been too long," Maddy said, feeling the warmth only an old friendship brings. "How are you and Randy getting along in your new home?"

Jodi had met Randy Gardner, a radio talk show host, the night she and Maddy attended a charity gala at The Glades. The event occurred before Maddy discovered the clever façade Avery Jordan and Naomi White had concocted to hide the place's perverse dark side.

"We're getting settled in pretty well. We like our jobs, and the area is outstanding. Are things well with you?"

She hesitated before answering. "Not really. I'm sorry to be calling with a problem, but you're someone I can talk with and trust."

"You don't need to explain; you know me better than that."

"I know, I know. It's just that it seems so crazy that I'm still haunted by what happened at The Glades."

"Are you kidding? What's going on?"

Maddy was at her kitchen table, and the end-of-day sun cast shadows outside when she began her story, but by the time she finished, it was dark. "It sounds like the girl who called you is in serious trouble. Have you ruled out going to the authorities?"

"I did that when Hector came to me for help to get his sister from the grips of The Glades. It took them too long to act, and she ended up dead. I don't know if I could have saved her, but if I had, she and Hector would be alive today."

"It's as though you're being drawn into something dangerous again. I can't believe this is happening to you; I'm so sorry. Are you thinking of going to Virginia?"

"I have to. I can't just turn my back; I'm not wired that way. The bad part is Adam won't know where I am because he's undercover, and I can't reach him. I also dare not blow up Amber's world with more craziness. She has enough on her mind. So, I'm turning to you, old friend; you're the only person other than me who will know where I am. I hate to ask this of you, but if something goes bad, you'll need to explain to them what happened to me on my behalf."

There was silence before Jodi said, "I wish I could go with you." Maddy knew she meant it. Jodi was fearless. She had been alone in Saigon when the North Vietnamese Army entered the city. Just ten years old, she found her way onto a helicopter to Cambodia and was adopted by an American family. Maddy never knew a more steadfast friend.

"I won't need to worry about explaining something going bad because I know you'll be okay," Jodi said. Maddy thanked her and said she'd keep her posted. When they hung up, she made flight arrangements for the following day.

She lay in bed that night, feeling she was handing her life over to fate. It was like entering a dark tunnel without knowing where it led. *My life's never been my own; it's always belonged to something greater than myself.* Holding her father's detective badge near, she whispered, "Dad, I'm entering an unknown and frightening place again; please be with me."

CHAPTER 9

Hannah Bates

Hannah sat straight in her chair, looking her boss in the eye as he challenged her judgment. "Special Agent in Charge Bates, why did you give Maddy Reynolds the Virginia address? You handle a critical operation, and until now, your performance has been stellar. This decision gives me pause about you." Chief Analyst Benjamin Harris was as crisp and seasoned an FBI agent as they came. He sat tall, trim, and firm-faced, gazing at Hannah over his reading glasses and holding a status report.

"Reynolds called me for the address. She was already on top of a place we'd been trying to locate for weeks. She's closer to our targets than we are. We'll monitor her whereabouts and reel her back if she gets too far out of reach."

"What makes you think she can handle herself with the people we're dealing with, Hannah? We don't need a dead noncombatant on our hands." Harris threw himself back in his seat, exasperated.

"I know Maddy Reynolds, Ben. She was an outstanding detective; she took out a serial killer and helped bring down Avery Jordan's operation at The Glades. I'd put her up against our best agents. And besides, had I not given her the information, she would have found it another way. At least now we're tracking her."

"I don't like it. I'm holding you responsible for Reynolds's safety. That will be all."

As she started for the door, Harris called to her. She stopped and turned. "I know all about Maddy Reynolds. I'm from Utica. The serial killer you're talking about killed my niece. I just want you to know that. It's easy to get caught up in the woman's reputation, but she's just flesh and blood. Be careful with her, Hannah. She doesn't hold back and will go for the jugular if she's backed into a corner. She's killed more bad guys than any agents on our team have arrested."

She gave him a slight nod and walked out. She returned to her desk and looked at the leafless maple trees lining the federal building entrance, casting end-of-day shadows on the faded lawn.

Hannah believed she knew Maddy better than anyone at the FBI. They'd worked together when an escaped con was coming to kill her. She had interrupted a retirement gathering for Maddy at her home. She had told her Jake Donnolly had escaped from Dannemora prison with the help of his brother Teddy and they were on their way to kill her. The woman's reaction was not what Hannah had expected. Reynolds had snapped, "What do you want me to do, run? If the Donnolly brothers want me, they know where to find me. I'm afraid that's all there is to it."

Hannah had thought Reynolds was foolish and full of bravado. She stormed out of the house, believing the woman was on her way to an early grave. Three months later, she was called to Maddy's mountain home late at night to find Jake Donnolly lying dead near the fireplace with his brains splattered over its lovely fieldstone. She had killed a man who loved to kill and whom other criminals feared. Hannah never underestimated Maddy Reynolds again.

Over time, a bond developed between them, or as much of a bond as two independent and headstrong women could forge. When she dug deep into Maddy's background, she found the saga of a little girl tormented by the ghost of her father's murderer. Deceived into believing the man died in prison, she discovered he'd come as Cupid to kill her, too.

People started leaving the building and walking to their cars. The December sun was setting, and it was time to go home. She packed her briefcase, and before leaving, she shuffled through a few messages that had come in while she met with her boss. One read, *Tell Hannah that Adam Forsyth called, and I'll try reaching her at another time.*

She moved slowly through rush hour traffic, thinking about the message. Adam had worked undercover for her when she was at the New York State Troopers, and she considered him a good cop. Like her, he'd been raising a teenager alone. But unlike her, he hadn't found a significant other after his wife died. The guy always seemed sad. She had a tender spot for Adam, and when he and Maddy met the night of the great fire and became an item, she couldn't think of a better match.

She knew what he'd have to say and dreaded the discussion. Adam was part of a law enforcement network where local FBI agents co-mingled with the troopers. She thought he knew Maddy's situation and wasn't happy about it.

I'm just doing my job. Over the years, she'd been called to make decisions that put her people at risk. For her, it always came down to the greater good. She knew it might seem hard-hearted to most people that she thought that way because it was like she was playing God. *I guess I am, but it has to be done.*

Her coworkers considered her a hard-ass. She thought it was because of her stoic expression, which she inherited from being the only girl among five brothers. *But there's a lot more going on inside that people don't see.*

As a kid, Hannah wasn't offered special consideration for being a girl. She had learned young to hit back hard. Her rugged exterior served her well throughout her career as she rose through the ranks in organizations of white men. She was a natural leader. Her ability to think quickly and make sound judgments helped her to stand out among her peers. But with Maddy Reynolds, she knew she was dealing with someone atypical. Like Ben had said, if forced into a corner, she'd kill or be killed, but wouldn't back down.

As she pulled into the driveway of her upscale suburban home, she thought of what awaited inside. When she crossed the threshold, she'd be stepping out of her role as Special Agent Hannah Bates and into the role of wife and mom. It was a magical transformation, and one she had never tired of.

After sitting with her husband and son for dinner, she got comfortable in the living room with her new book, *Beloved.* Anthony, her husband, had volunteered to clean up in the kitchen and her son went to his room to study. Her mind drifted from the words on the page to Reynolds and what she might learn while in Virginia. She knew Maddy wouldn't relent. *She'll dig as far as she can, and if she digs too deep, she might get herself killed.*

CHAPTER 10

Maddy

It feels strange to be in Washington again so soon. Her flight arrived before noon, and unlike when she came for the conference, she didn't know what she'd be doing. She rented a car and started on the thirty-minute drive to Arlington, Virginia. When she was close, she pulled into a gas station, grabbed the map, and penciled out a route to Bleeker Road.

It appeared like Anywhere, USA when she got close and started looking for the house. She found it, and the place was a plain ranch. It stood among similar cookie-cutter dwellings, with its curtains drawn and an empty driveway. She drove around the block to view it from the back. The yard was barren, with not even a picnic table.

She pulled over when she returned to the front and parked a few houses down the street. A woman sat outside on the stoop of the house next door, reading a magazine and looking at two little girls riding tricycles in the driveway.

Maddy walked past the children and up the steps to 944. She listened for sounds inside, but there were none. The mailbox was empty, and unlike the other houses, it had no lawn chairs on its concrete porch to sit. Before knocking, she glanced over at the woman watching the toddlers, but with her head buried in the magazine, she seemed unaware Maddy was there. She knocked and waited. No answer. She tried turning the doorknob, but it didn't budge. *Shit!*

She glanced at the woman again, who now was gazing at her. "I wonder if you can help me." The woman put the magazine on her lap and looked over.

Maddy walked to her, stopped about ten feet away, and said her girlfriend lived next door and had asked her to come and pick her up. Now Maddy was shooting in the dark. "She's Asian and in her twenties. Do you know her?"

The woman stood up. "Kim-Ly? Sure, I know Kim." Maddy walked closer and introduced herself. She said her name was Cathy. The two little girls looked on, straddling their tricycles, and she added, "These are my girls, Tara and Brandi." She smiled at them, and the thought of being a grandmother in a few years flashed through her head.

"Have you seen Kim?"

"Not for over a week. Her friend hasn't been around either. He usually comes by every other day."

She said Kim had sent her a key a while back, but she misplaced it. "I think she left me a note inside. You wouldn't have a key to the place, would you?"

"Yes, she left me one. Hang on, I'll get it." She told her girls to stay with Maddy and as Maddy waited, she asked which was Tara and which was Brandi.

"I'm Brandi," the bigger child said. "My sister is Tara. She's shy; she don't talk to people she don't know." The girls were adorable, and the thought she might have a couple of grandkids in a few years made her feel old. *I'm not ready for that.*

Cathy returned, handed Maddy a key, and asked her to bring it back before leaving. When she went to the house and opened the door, Maddy entered a room without furniture. The place was stark – no pictures, rugs, or accessories. The kitchen was barren except for two wine glasses on the counter. She opened the refrigerator, and four bottles of wine and a dish of dried-up strawberries sat alone with no other food. *I think I'm getting the picture.*

One of the two bedrooms was empty, and a queen-size bed in the other room was made up. A lamp and a telephone sat on a bedside cabinet. The top cabinet drawer contained a stack of papers. As she shuffled through, she became conscious of time. She folded the stack, shoved them into her back pocket, and pulled her shirt over. In the bottom drawer, she found a half-empty box of condoms. *Kim and her friend are using the place to shack up.*

Before leaving, she left a note on the kitchen counter. *Kim, I was here. Call my home. I'll keep checking for messages. Maddy Reynolds.* As she walked to her car, she stopped, returned the key, and told Cathy there was no note. "I may stop back again. Thanks, and have a good day."

She knew what she did was deceptive and illegal, but believed the girl was in trouble and needed help. When she left Bleeker, she drove to a Marriott she'd spotted on the way and got a room for the night. She plopped herself on a bed, gazing at the ceiling with her heart pounding, wondering what she was getting herself into. She lay still, tried to calm down, then got up and pulled out the papers she had taken. Setting them on the desk, she looked down at them, afraid of what they might tell her.

Before sitting, she grabbed a bottle of wine she'd brought in her suitcase, opened it, and poured the pinot into a hotel glass. She sat and began reading. Loose-leaf papers, notes, and a few business cards were crumpled together, along with four matching receipts from Bayside Housing. Each receipt was for twelve hundred dollars. All were rent invoices for the house and were addressed to Gerald Ellis.

Holy shit! Ellis was Kim-Ly's lover. It was as though she'd connected a couple of dots. There were several sheets of loose-leaf paper with notes such as, *See you Thursday*, *miss you*, and, *please don't call my house.* But one got Maddy's full attention. It read, *I think Steven knows.* Maddy wondered if Steven was her husband. *Maybe, but it just doesn't feel right.*

One business card was for Red Eye Taxi Service, and the other was for Girard's on the River Walk in San Antonio. She wondered if Girard's on the River Walk was connected to Darius Girard, who had worked at The Glades. She dialed the number on the card. A woman answered, and she asked for Darius. When the woman said she'd get him, Maddy hung up. *This is getting weird.*

As she thumbed through the paperwork, a photo of a man with his arm around a pretty Asian woman dropped out. They stood on a boardwalk on a sunny day. The man looked like the guy she had seen dead in the street, and the girl seemed familiar, but she couldn't place her.

She couldn't stop thinking, and her mind was charging forward like an out-of-control locomotive on a downhill track. *Gerald Ellis was working on sex trafficking; he was having an affair with the woman who called me for help two days after his death, and it looked like he'd been to San Antonio to visit Darius Girard at his restaurant.* Like she was putting together a puzzle, she held the pieces in place within her mind, waiting for connections to be made. *I need more information*, she thought.

She had come to Virginia to find a girl in trouble, but things had gotten more complex. It made no sense to wait for Kim-Ly to show up at 944; the girl wasn't returning to the house now that her lover was dead. Maddy followed her instincts; the only card in her hand to play was in San Antonio. She rearranged her flight schedule and continued trying to unravel the mystery while she was in the air, but no matter how she put it together, the puzzle pieces didn't fit.

CHAPTER 11

It was eighty-eight degrees, sunny, and a little past noon when Maddy arrived in San Antonio. Before heading out to find Girard's, she checked into the Holiday Inn near the River Walk and showered. She had never been to San Antonio and felt enamored with the area's low-key ambiance. Music playing, kids moving by on skateboards, and people walking dogs reminded her of summer in a park with her parents when she was little.

The sign for Girard's restaurant was lit with blue cursive letters, nestled in a bend along the river. She walked in and sat at an open table. As she absorbed the assembly of abstract art pieces mounted on the walls, a beautiful, dark-skinned server with hooped gold earrings came by and asked what she'd like to drink.

"Well, this is my first time in San Antonio. What do you recommend?"

"My favorite is the house michelada."

"Then, michelada, it is," she said. She had tried to determine how to best approach Darius Girard while on the airplane but remained unsure. When the woman returned with her drink, she sipped the michelada and began considering her options. *I could be very direct, go for the throat, and try to intimidate him into telling me what he knows about the girl.* Her gut told her hardball wasn't the way to go with Darius. She thought he was rational and gentle and should be approached with reason. When the server passed by again, she asked if Darius was in.

"He's in the kitchen."

"Can you tell him an old friend is here and ask him to come out?" The last time she saw the man, Jordan held her hostage at The Glades. Darius had seemed repulsed by what Jordan and Neri had done, but didn't do anything about it.

He rushed out of the kitchen, wiping his hands with a towel, and froze when he saw Maddy. The tall, thin, bald-headed man looked as if he was in shock. She smiled. "Hello, Darius. It's been a while." He plodded to the table and sat down. He seemed as tight as an unopened ketchup bottle top, looking off to the side as if waiting to be scolded.

"I love your restaurant; it looks like you've started a new life." He nodded, said yes, and nothing more. Tension, like static electricity, emanated between them. Trying to think of something to say to help the guy relax, she asked if he would feel more comfortable talking while walking along the river. He nodded and said he would.

The sun had gone behind a cloud as they walked, and a slight breeze kicked up. She said she wasn't there to cause him any harm.

"I have a wife and two sons. I'm trying to put The Glades behind me, and all I want is to be left to live my life. I'm not involved in that world anymore."

"Have you heard about the government probe into sex trafficking?" He said he had. "It's stirring up a hornets' nest, and even though you've put The Glades behind, The Glades hasn't done the same for you. I'm here because I need to know what Gerald Ellis discussed when he came to see you."

He stopped walking. "I haven't gotten a visit from anyone with that name. I don't know a Gerald Ellis."

She believed him, but she sensed someone else had visited. She put on her actress hat and said, "Then who was it who came here?" He looked away. "Darius, I'm not here to cause you harm," she reiterated. "I'm trying to help a girl, and anything you can tell me may save her life. Start doing the right thing if you want to put that world behind you."

He turned, looked at her, and said, "Naomi White."

Naomi fucking White! Maddy screeched to herself. Her purpose in San Antonio had just changed. With her fists clenched, she said, "Now is the time to step away from your past, Darius, and build the future you seek. Tell me what Naomi wanted."

He sighed and leaned back on a nearby tree. "There's a lot you don't know. Avery Jordan had deep ties to the underworld. They've been silent for three years, but with the onset of the sex trafficking probe, they have reemerged and want the ledger. If they don't get it, Naomi will be dead. She's very motivated, and I don't need to tell you how cunning and ruthless she can be."

Confused, Maddy asked, "What is the ledger?"

"It was Jordan's bible. He kept the names of every person who visited The Glades and their purchases." She felt like she might vomit. Everything just changed again. A document with the names of influential men who enslaved young girls for sexual pleasure was an atom bomb. The faces of the woman she'd seen auctioned off during the masquerade event flashed before her.

"Can we sit?" she asked, feeling woozy. They walked to a bench near the water's edge and sat down. She sighed and asked him to explain everything he knew about the ledger.

"Jordan alone handled it, and it never left his office. I'd see it when he'd take it out of his wall safe and sometimes on his desk. He often used it to call potential clients and determine who might attend an event. It identified every person who visited The Glades. It also contained the number of women each man purchased and the transaction amount."

"When was it seen last?"

"Naomi saw it on Avery's desk an hour before the fire."

"Well, it burned in the fire, don't you think?"

"The ledger had a tungsten crest on its cover, and according to Naomi, they didn't find it in the evidence vault, which means it still exists."

"Someone got into the evidence vault? Who could do that?"

"Like I said, the mafiosos involved are powerful, connected, and ruthless. Jordan was afraid of them, and now, so is Naomi. She's desperate, which makes her very dangerous."

"Did Naomi have a theory about what happened to it?"

"She thinks the Lemont kid took it. She said he had a paper bag under his arm when she shot him."

With that, Maddy had to work at not vomiting. *Hector?* She sat back in her chair, watching the river drift. It seemed so peaceful, so calm. She struggled to grasp the enormity of the situation, thinking of men preying on the innocent at The Glades and the boy dear to her heart who died trying to stop it.

She stood, gave him an appreciative look, and, before leaving, asked about his family. He said he and his wife married five years ago and had one-year-old and two-year-old sons. "Love them up. They'll grow before you know it." She put out her hand. "Goodbye, Darius." They left each other, walking in opposite directions.

CHAPTER 12

Maddy's flight back to Syracuse from San Antonio seemed like an eternity. Darius Girard had blown up her idea of what she was dealing with. A document containing the names of powerful men involved in sex slavery was like combining the ingredients of nitroglycerin, creating a volatile situation. Her mind raced as she began reassessing the situation.

What are you going to do, Maddy? Do you think you can back out of the coming storm? Quit bullshitting yourself. You're going to war, and someone will die; isn't that how it always is? She'd been fighting, facing that something was coming since she saw Gerald Ellis lying in the street. She had wanted to hold on to her three-year respite, but it was futile. *There will be no peaceful outcome with Naomi White in the picture.*

Frank Zepatello's words popped into her head; *Denial gets you dead, Maddy.* He was her boss at the Oneida County Sheriff's Office when she started as a detective. As an army captain in Vietnam, he led his detectives as though they were a unit at war. He was tough as nails, but Maddy wouldn't have traded his leadership for any wishy-washy types she'd seen. "When you're in battle," he would tell her, "look everywhere, question everything, and think before doing anything. Respond, never react. Always beware of denial; denial gets you dead."

She talked in her mind with her friend, mentor, and the person who insisted she'd be the first woman detective in the department. *I guess I'm in the shit again, Zep.* Lost in her thoughts, she noticed a little girl about seven across the aisle gazing at her, pigtails tied with pink bows and a beaming smile. Her brown eyes lit up her pretty black face as she lifted a hand and squeezed it several times to say hello. Maddy smiled and realized the child and others like her were why she needed to enter the fight.

She remembered finding Sarah Benning's body in a portable toilet at a construction site. Sarah was not much older than the girl across the aisle. Cupid, a demented serial killer, had raped and strangled the child. Maddy never understood why she had entered the world of exploited girls and women. It was like Sidney Myers had told her, "Trying to understand why your life is what it is, is like trying to empty the ocean into a bucket; it's just too damn big." She didn't figure it out anymore; she just did what she had to do, and what she had to do now was follow the mystery.

It was almost 2:30 AM when she inched up the road to her house. Exhausted and ready to drop when she stepped inside, she glanced at the message machine, but the light wasn't blinking. Leaving her luggage unpacked, she slipped off her clothes and crawled into bed.

The following day, she was up just before noon. It was cold inside her place; she put on warm clothes and went to the kitchen to start the coffee. Quarter-size snowflakes fell. *It's beautiful.* The coffee finished, she poured a cup and settled in a comfortable chair in the living room, thinking about the girl. *Kim-Ly is her name. What a pretty name. I hope she calls me again.*

Then her mind went to the ledger. *Until yesterday, I didn't know the damn thing existed; now, it's the key to everything.* She tried retracing how she and Adam came down the mountain the night The Glades burned. *We followed Hector's blood trail to Route 3 and ended up at Doc's house. It was dark when we found him; the ledger would have been easy to overlook.*

But why did he take it in the first place? Maddy knew the boy wouldn't have understood what the ledger was. All she could figure was Hector thought it looked important, and if it went missing, it would harm Jordan.

The state police had treated the house like a crime scene and spent hours inside. If the ledger was there, they should have found it. Yet they weren't looking for anything specific, so maybe they didn't search throughout the house. Then again, maybe Hector dropped it on his way down the mountain.

She couldn't tie together all the unanswered questions. All she knew for sure was Darius Girard said the ledger contained the names of all who took part in sex trafficking at The Glades, and the underworld bosses knew it existed. *They'll stop at nothing to find it, and now that Naomi White's life is on the line, she'll be as dangerous as Sedgwick Neri.* She also believed Naomi would think Maddy might know where it was. *I wonder how she'll come at me?*

Maddy wanted to check out Doc's place. She needed to speak with Jason alone and remembered Miranda saying she had Thursday afternoons off. *That's where I'm headed this afternoon.* It was Thursday, and she didn't want to wait another week.

She went outside to clear snow from her Jeep and noticed tracks. She walked over, and giant bear prints came from the woods and crossed the field behind her house. *That damn thing's a monster,* she thought. *I better make a trip to the landfill soon.*

On her way to the village, Maddy stopped at Things Forgotten to check on her coffee mug order before stopping to see Jason. Julie Barnes looked up from her chair behind the front counter when she walked in. "Oh, I can't believe your timing. Your order came in yesterday."

Julie lifted a box from behind the counter, pulled back its cardboard flaps, and six French brass coffee mugs lay packed in tissue paper. She handed one to Maddy. "Wow, perfect. They're heavy, aren't they?" She lifted it and let it drop in her hand a few times, then handed it back to Julie. "Would you gift wrap them for me?"

"Sure." Julie brought the box to the back room while Maddy browsed the store. As she moved past a shelf of interesting-looking figurines, one seemed out of place. It was a ballerina made of brass. It stood on one toe in a tutu. The brass seemed weathered, and something sad about it spoke to her like it had an untold story.

She brought it to the counter and said the ballerina caught her eye when Julie came out. "It's unusual, isn't it?"

"It's more than unusual; it's a mystery." Julie took it into her hands, cradled it, and her face filled with wonder. "This was a precious family keepsake. It belonged to Ester Lemont. Her mother had given it to her, and she gave it to Anna Jean; God rest her soul. Hector told me A.J. brought it with her when she moved to The Glades."

Maddy's heart dropped, knowing the sorrows of the Lemont family. She needed to learn more. "How did it get here?"

"That's the mystery. About a week after the fire at The Glades, a couple of boys brought it here and wanted me to buy it for five dollars. I recognized it because Ester wanted to sell it to me when she needed money for food. I told her I wouldn't buy it, but I'd give her a loan, and she could pay it when her situation improved."

Maddy asked where the boys had found it. "They said it was on the side of the road near the bottom of The Glades mountain. Maybe I shouldn't tell you this, but dried blood covered the ballerina." In an instant, Maddy knew what had happened. *Hector had to have carried it with him down the mountain after being shot. He would have walked down the road to Doc's house. He was bleeding, he was weak, and it must have fallen.* She realized he may have had the ledger, too.

"Are you okay, Maddy?"

She nodded. "How much for the ballerina?"

"You can have it; I can't take money for that."

After paying Julie for the mugs, she carried the ballerina with the wrapped box of coffee mugs to the Jeep. She placed the items on the passenger seat, covered her face, and, thinking of the sad plight of the Lemont family, wept.

It was as though the anguish from three years earlier had been waiting for her. *Sorrow needs to see the light of day,* she thought to herself as she sat with tears streaming down her face, watching townspeople going about their business, walking up and down Main Street in the snow. She cleaned her face with a tissue, caught her breath, and started for Jason's.

She carried the box with the mugs inside as Jason sat signing papers at the front desk. "Maddy Reynolds, how are you?" he said with a beaming smile as he walked around to greet her. She handed him the gift and said it was a little something for his practice.

"You shouldn't have." She prompted him to open it, and he pulled out a mug, examining its unusual style. "Oh, my, they're beautiful. I can use these, thank you." He gestured to a sofa in the seating area. "Let's sit."

She asked how the new medical practice was going, and he said he didn't realize how much the town needed local medical services. "My father must have been busy."

"Everyone thought well of your dad. I'm sure you'll do well." Trying to figure out a way to get around to the ledger, she said, "You mentioned you wanted to know about events that led to your dad's death. Is this a good time?"

He said he had no patients for the rest of the day. "How about I make us a pot of coffee? We'll try out the new mugs."

When Jason went to the kitchen, she noticed the medicine cabinet where she found the Demerol she used to kill Neri. She remembered struggling to find a syringe in the dark as Neri picked himself off the floor before charging at her. It was before he slashed her back with his razor-sharp knife. Just the thought brought a jolt of pain to her lower back.

He returned with two steamy, hot mugs of coffee and sat across from her. "There is so much about my father's last years that I don't know. We lost touch while I was in med school; believe it or not, he never got to meet Cecilia after we got engaged."

She told him how she first met his father amidst a medical crisis. "Hector Lemont was stacking wood at my house when a bee stung him, and he had an allergic reaction. I had just moved to the area, and he struggled to tell me how to find your father's practice. He was unconscious when I got here."

Sipping her coffee, thinking about how helpless she felt as the boy faded off to near death, she said, "But your dad, as cool as can be, lifted him out of my truck and carried him inside. He administered epinephrine, and Hector came out of it. While we waited for the boy to come around, your father and I chatted. It didn't take long to realize he was a wonderful man."

"I understand he had strong feelings about The Glades, even before the fire."

"He had a keen sixth sense," Maddy said. "He suspected Luellen Hicks's death was murder. They found her dead in the woods with her throat cut." She explained how the police said it was suicide, but Doc knew how improbable it was for a woman to kill herself that way. "Your dad had become suspicious that the sheriff was on Avery Jordan's payroll."

She explained how things deteriorated during that summer. "The Glades seemed to creep up on me, unexpected. I didn't realize that my moving here triggered Jordan's paranoia. He thought I was still in law enforcement and was working undercover."

"One day, and I'll never forget it, I came back to my place from the village and found my house trashed. I couldn't believe it. 'Why would anyone do this?' I wondered. When I searched my home, I found an electronic bug inside my phone; the local cops were listening in on my calls. I didn't know what was happening and didn't know where to turn. The only person I knew here was your dad, so I went to him."

Jason's eyes seemed glued on her as she spoke; he'd hardly touched his coffee. "I can't believe I didn't know all this was happening. I was so wrapped up in my little med school world, I didn't even realize my father needed me. Please, keep going."

"I could tell he was concerned about the danger we were putting ourselves in by talking about Jordan and The Glades. He asked to meet at the end of a muddy road late at night; it was rainy and murky. He knew he was putting himself in danger, but he met with me, anyway."

She felt like she was sitting in her car with Doc, just like that night. She looked at the snow falling outside. "When your dad told me about the Hicks girl, he said the sheriff and all his cronies were on Jordan's payroll. He also thought I was a target and my life was in danger." She sighed, looked at

Jason, and added, "When he left my car, it was the last anyone saw him alive."

Jason looked down and shook his head. "I wish I had been here for him." She didn't try to talk him out of his feelings of regret because she knew it was impossible. When he looked back at her, she continued.

"The police records said he drove off into the bluff because of a poorly marked guard rail. A few days later, I returned to the scene and found glass from a broken taillight seventy feet from where he went off. It wasn't an accident. They murdered your dad by forcing him off the road."

"The story I was told never made sense to me. My father was the slowest, most cautious driver I ever knew." He looked at Maddy and added, "I needed to know this."

"There's something more I want to discuss with you, Jason." He looked at her. "The night of the fire, Naomi White killed Hector Lemont. I found him on a sofa right here in this house. He had descended the mountain with a gunshot wound."

"The thing is, I believe he was carrying a rather important document. It's a ledger containing the names of the men who participated in the goings-on at The Glades. Not only does it include the names of attendees, but information about the girls they purchased. Many of them may still live as sex slaves."

Jason looked at her as if watching an Alfred Hitchcock horror flick. "The ledger wasn't found. The people who knew of it thought it burned in the fire. It's come to light that the ledger exists. Now dangerous people are after it. Hector may have hidden it somewhere in this house before he died." He looked at her like he wasn't sure what she wanted him to do. "When you moved in, what did you do with your father's belongings?"

"We boxed everything up and put it in the basement. We meant to have it carted out but haven't gotten around to it."

"Would you mind if I come here when you're not seeing patients so I can examine the basement?"

"By all means. But there's a ton of stuff in those boxes, and it might take a while. Sundays would be best." Maddy stood to leave, looked at Jason, and felt the same warm feeling she had with his father. As she drove home, she felt like a detective again and remembered something Hannah Bates had told her about herself years earlier. *Once a detective, always a detective, right Maddy?*

When she got home, she brought the ballerina to a shelf near the fireplace and placed it on the mantle.

CHAPTER 13

Hannah

Hannah sat at her desk in Albany's FBI office, poring over old reports on The Glades, looking for nuggets that might reveal new information about its shady past. The phone rang, and Ethan Grant, an agent who assisted her on the case, was on the other end. "What's the latest?" she asked.

"Reynolds visited the Arlington address we gave her, and she changed her flight before she left the DC area. Instead of returning to Syracuse, she flew to San Antonio. She checked into a hotel, headed for the River Walk, and visited Girard's, a restaurant owned by Darius Girard from The Glades. They strolled together along the river, talking."

"Do you know what they discussed?"

"Our soundman couldn't get much; there was a lot of background noise. But the word 'ledger' came up a few times."

"Ledger? What the hell does that mean?"

"We don't know."

"Stay with it, please, Ethan." She hung up and looked out the window at the gray day. *Ledger,* she thought. *Really?* The word rattled around in her head; she scribbled it on a sheet of paper, retracing it repeatedly. Then, for the hell of it, she grabbed a dictionary and looked it up. It read, *A book or other collection of financial accounts of a particular type.*

Wait, a minute! She pushed the intercom button. "Bring the preliminary Suarez report." She got up and began pacing the room with her hands behind her back as she waited, trying to recall something she'd read. The congressman's staff put together the report to support a rationale for the investigation.

The assistant brought in the hefty document and laid it on a table. Hannah began thumbing through. *There it is!* She began reading the excerpt aloud. "'As with any extensive business where sizable sums of money transfer hands, written records exist. Organized criminal enterprises must use business principles to function. Otherwise, limited by their inefficiencies, they operate from one transaction to the next. Therefore, the magnitude and scale of The Glades's business must have had a source document for its financial transactions that might include its patrons' names.'"

"Holy shit." She picked up the phone and called Harris. "It's Hannah here, Ben. We believe a document containing financial activity at The Glades exists. It might include names."

"Do we have any idea where it is?" His voice had an intensity unusual for the controlled man.

"Not yet. It's most likely in Berry Lake."

"Damn, that'll shake the acorns from the trees. Once it gets out that it exists, anyone who's ever been to the place will look for it. How did we find out?"

"Reynolds."

"Great. That puts her in the middle of a shitstorm. Do we have any of our people in Berry Lake?"

"No, the town is too small. People would recognize them."

"Jesus, this isn't good, Hannah. Reynolds is in the eye of the storm. They'll be coming after her now. I hope she has her bag of tricks ready because she'll need it to get out of this one unscathed." Hannah didn't say anything, but she knew he was right.

"Now I have something for you. I just got a call from the troopers. Forsyth has gone deep. They think he's penetrated one of the mob's inner circles, but they're not sure who the guys are. They don't think they'll hear from him again until this is over. There are a lot of moving parts here; let's hope we don't lose any."

Hannah crossed her arms when they hung up, deep in thought. She leaned back against the desk, wondering what Adam might be into. It seemed serendipitous that he and Maddy were in the same drama, unbeknownst to one another.

She started thinking about when they became an item. *They seemed so perfect for each other. Maddy, a longtime divorced woman, strong-willed, with a sadness that hung near the surface, and Adam, a widower, kind and understanding; it just couldn't have been any better,* she thought. *It will be awful if they're caught in the same funnel cloud, spinning into a tornado's death zone.*

A macabre thought struck her. *It would be better if neither makes it out alive rather than just one.* She couldn't imagine one going on without the other. The sad notion brought tears to her eyes, and she thought, *They've had three years of happiness; maybe that's all anyone's allowed.*

CHAPTER 14

Maddy

It was Saturday morning, and it was cold but sunny. Maddy called Lester's hardware store and asked if he had access to a metal detector. "Sure, we rent detectors. Lots of folks around here look for relics from the French and Indian War." When she asked whether they detected titanium, he told her to hang on and that he'd check. When he returned, he said they did.

"Can you hold one for me? I'll swing by to get it later."

She dug out her warmest clothes and a pair of hiking boots she had bought when she first moved to Berry Lake and readied herself for an afternoon in the woods. She arrived at Lester's a little before noon, and the device lay on the counter when she walked in. "I checked it out, and it's in good working order."

She noticed a television turned to CNN on the counter that hadn't been there before and asked him when he got cable. "Just last week. I figure it'll break up the monotony on slow days."

"What are you trying to find with the detector?" he asked as he handed over an aluminum rod with an oblong plate at the bottom and a meter below its hand grip. She didn't want to endanger her friend by giving him information someone might kill for, so she said remnants from The Glades fire. "Well, I rent it by the hour. We can square up later."

She left the store and drove to the foot of The Glades mountain, and her thoughts returned to the night years earlier when the sky glowed red and an inferno threatened to melt everything in its path. She had realized people were dying and remembered worrying Hector might be one. The experience still lived within her, and her mind returned to that night again. She pulled over next to the *Welcome to Berry Lake* sign and started up the hill.

Transported back in time, she was with Adam, engulfed in a wall of flames. The heat descended, smoke swirled in the wind, and trees crashed to earth, exploding tiny embers into the air. The fire's rumbling sounded like a freight train, and the night was alive with death.

She stopped, leaned against a tree, and returned to the present. *Man, I wasn't expecting that.* Starting up the hill again, she recalled the approximate path she and Adam had descended that night. They had been confident it was the way Hector traveled because smatterings of his blood marked the way.

Moving the detector about, it beeped fifty yards in. Kicking dirt around, she pulled up a large rusty nail. Holding it in her palm, she shook her head and thought, *I hope there aren't many more like this, or it'll take forever to scan the side of this mountain.*

Continuing to wave the device from side to side, she moved forward and recognized a flat area where blood had soaked a swath of ground. Heavy in the heart and hollow in the stomach, she sat on a fallen tree, feeling all over again what it was like when she first realized Hector might die.

Her mind was half in the present and half in the past as she moved upward, over creeks, mud, and rock beds. When she reached the foot of a ridge, she stopped. She smiled. It was the spot where Adam had made a joke after sliding down the slippery hill. *It was the moment I let him into my heart.* She remembered thinking that he was someone who walked into an inferno with her to save a boy he'd never met, and at that moment, she realized he was special.

The metal detector began beeping. Excited, Maddy kicked at the mud until her foot hit a hard object. She scratched, pulled, and yanked until something the size of a hand tool broke loose. Caked in mud, she brought it to a nearby stream to wash it off. It was a .32-caliber revolver. *Holy shit. This is Adam's; he lost it when he fell.* Gazing at the weapon, thinking of how the fateful night brought her to the man who became her lover, she began missing him. She pushed forward.

Near the top of the mountain, the beeping became constant. She dug up nails, aluminum ductwork, parts of steel doors, and unrecognizable remnants of The Glades. They were shrapnel from the mighty explosion that rocked the night when something inside ignited.

She realized finding the ledger that way was futile. She turned and started back down. At her vehicle, she kicked the mud from her boots, lay the metal detector in the back of the Jeep, and headed back to Lester's. When she entered the hardware store, Lester was in the back room, so she waited for him at the counter.

Half paying attention to CNN, an unmistakable effervescent voice captured her attention. She turned, and a woman with Coke-bottle-thick eyeglasses and spaghetti-straight hair talked with reporters.

It was Cynthia Morgan, Senator Winthrop's assistant. When a reporter asked about Senator Winthrop's recent election victory, the woman seemed full of herself as she spouted off about his commitment to tearing down barriers and building bridges among diverse groups of people.

Something about her seemed phony, and Maddy was about to tune her out when she noticed an Asian girl who looked similar to Kim-Ly standing with a group who appeared to be part of the Winthrop team. *Can it be?* She opened her purse and pulled out the photo of the girl and Gerald Ellis standing on a boardwalk. *Son of a bitch, it's her!* She glared at the TV, flabbergasted, unable to connect the dots.

Distracted when Lester walked out and asked if she'd found anything, she said she hadn't found anything of great interest. She kept her eyes glued to the television.

Preoccupied, wondering what Kim-Ly was doing with Cynthia Morgan, she paid for the detector and left. Befuddled and feeling she needed to catch up with her thoughts, she pulled off onto a dirt road that led to the lake and drove to the water's edge. The water glittered in the afternoon sun. Looking across the shimmer, trying to figure out what was happening, she listed each factor as though she were adding numbers in a simple math equation.

Cynthia Morgan is Senator Winthrop's assistant; I got that. Kim-Ly was Gerald Ellis's lover. He was investigating sex trafficking; I got that too. Ellis contacted me for information about my experience at The Glades, a sex trafficking operation. So far, so good.

Here's where it gets dicey. Kim-Ly reached out to me for help just after someone killed her lover. Why? What was she afraid of? How did she get involved with Gerald Ellis? Why is she with Cynthia Morgan, Winthrop's assistant? There's a missing piece here that ties this all together. What is it?

Something was moving inside of her. She sat on the shore, tossing pebbles into the water, wracking her brain, trying to pinpoint what she'd overlooked. Then it hit her. *Oh, my God, the sex auction! Kim was among the girls that were purchased. That's how I recognize her.*

She picked up a rock, threw it, and when it landed with a splash, she yelled, "Asshole!" Maddy realized Kim-Ly was Senator Winthrop's sex slave. She started going to a dark place of indignation and rage within herself. It was a place built each time she witnessed an attack by powerful people on the innocent.

Her mind flashed back to the Washington conference, thinking, *Miss fucking goody-two-shoes, Cynthia Morgan, dares to stand in front of all those helping professionals and spew out her horseshit about how Winthrop is a champion for behavioral health sciences.* She clenched her fists and screamed, "He has a fucking sex slave!"

Her words echoed throughout the vast space as she cried for justice to the ancient mountains looking on. *It's as though they know,* she thought. She looked up at the tallest where The Glades once stood, and the sickness she felt the night of the sex slave auction poured back into her spirit; she shuddered.

Drained of strength, sickened by the foulness of injustice at the highest level of government, Maddy started for her vehicle and headed for her house. Still in disbelief, when she walked into her place, she saw the message light blinking; it was her daughter.

"Mom, you're not returning my calls. Is everything alright? Please call me." Tempted to pick up the phone, Maddy balked. *I can't talk to her now. I can't hide my feelings; if she knows what's going on, I'll blow up her world.* She sat, put her head in her hands, and wondered what she would do.

Maddy had gotten used to operating alone after leaving the sheriff's department. The entire experience confronting Avery Jordan she'd handled on her own. But this was too big, and she wanted her detective friends, Zep, Al, and Bud, with her at that moment. She looked at the phone, picked up the receiver, and dialed the Oneida County Sheriff's detective unit.

"Zepatello, here."

"Hi, it's Maddy."

"Maddy, what's wrong?" Zep knew something wasn't right. He'd known her through the early years when she held nothing back. He knew her when she was strong, and he knew her when she doubted herself. Zep was one of the few people with whom Maddy allowed herself to be vulnerable.

"I think I'm over my head, Zep. I can't say much; I fear they compromised my phone. But I'm in shit again and about to jump in deep." She knew he understood. No further explanation was required. She listened as he spoke. It was like he was talking to one of his soldiers in Vietnam, about to go on a dangerous mission.

"Maddy, you graduated to solo a long time ago. Look into yourself; remember the battles you've fought and the lessons they've taught you. Keep your head up when it needs to be up and down when it needs to be down. Remember, trust your intuition."

He paused. She could hear him moving about his office with the phone as he always did, thinking as he spoke. "I wish I could be with you in whatever you're facing, but you are way out of my jurisdiction." His voice wavered, then softened. "Hang tough, Maddy. I'll be praying for you."

After they hung up, she thought of things he had said to her about going into battle over the years. When she started as a detective, he told her how certain soldiers would graduate to solo in Vietnam. They'd volunteered for reconnaissance missions and worked alone. They were the bravest, most confident, and most skilled. He'd told her she was that type when she killed Cupid.

She went to the window that overlooked the lake and looked out; the sun had set, and the sky was purple. It was the gloaming. She had tried to extricate herself from an incredible drama, but it was like swimming upriver; she'd made little progress.

It's not just about me. It's about the girls sold at The Glades and other places like it; it must stop. Feeling at peace, as though she accepted her role in the unfolding drama, she picked up the phone and made flight arrangements to Washington, DC for the following day.

CHAPTER 15

It was late morning when she arrived in DC. After renting a car, Maddy drove to the Russell Senate Building on Capitol Hill, where Winthrop had his offices. She found a coffee shop near the lobby and readied herself for a long stint of waiting. People walked in and out of the building, shaping ideas to lead the nation. She disdained their high-mindedness, knowing how a senator had betrayed the people's trust.

She watched for Winthrop or his assistant. According to the schedule, he was to attend a Children and Families Committee meeting at two o'clock, and she had hoped he would return to his office when it ended.

Kim's voice played in her head as she waited. *I'm afraid for my life.* Maddy's strategy was to remain clandestine, follow Winthrop to his residence, and from that point, ad-lib, hoping to steal the girl away. Anyone following a senator to his home was a security threat, and she knew she was putting herself at risk, yet it was a chance worth taking to save the girl.

At 4:20, after three Cokes and two trips to the bathroom, she heard Cynthia Morgan's unmistakable cackle echoing through the lobby. Morgan walked alongside two men without the Senator. Engrossed in conversation, they disappeared into an elevator. She paid her tab, went to her vehicle, and waited. Within minutes, Morgan stepped outside with another woman, who looked like Kim, and hailed a cab. She followed.

It was a windy November afternoon, and the traffic was thick with government workers trying to get out of town for the weekend. She stayed close. The taxi pulled over near a paid parking area, and she did the same. Cynthia carried a briefcase as Kim followed her into the parking lot. They drove out in a white Saab, and Maddy followed at a distance.

The Saab hit Route 270, heading northwest. It was already dark, and she closed the gap to keep from losing it. She wondered where Morgan was going as the headlights of other vehicles grew fewer and fewer, and the Saab kept heading north. Thirty minutes beyond Frederick, Maryland, Morgan pulled off onto a dirt road, and Maddy continued straight, fearing if she didn't, Morgan might identify her. "Shit," she yelled, thinking she'd lost her.

She pulled into an abandoned gas station a half mile down the road. She tried to determine her next move and realized the chances of finding the Saab in the dark were slim. She turned around, headed back to the same dirt road, took a right, and found herself in a treed area with hills. There were no houses within the first quarter mile.

She noticed a house's lights. A sizable rustic log structure in a ravine on her right had a single vehicle in its circular driveway, but its make was unclear. She continued another eighth of a mile; the road ended, and the house in the ravine was the only home on the road.

She turned around, pulled over, and shut off the car's engine and lights. *It's dark, I'm fifty yards away from the house, and there's a steep decline with lots of trees and brush to navigate.* Her thoughts went round and round but ended up in the same place. *It all adds up to getting out and moving down the road.* She walked the road toward the driveway in the dark, but fearing anyone looking through a window would see her, she stepped into the woods when she neared the home.

She walked over branches and rocks, with only the slightest light illuminating from within the house windows. Headlights appeared. She crouched down and hoped the driver hadn't seen her silhouette. As a car turned into the driveway, she peeked and watched a large Mercedes-Benz crawl to a stop behind the Saab. A man got out carrying an overnight bag and walked inside.

That has to be Winthrop. She inched her way around the side of the house. Of the three windows, there was light in one, and when she reached it, she looked in and saw two women, Cynthia and Kim.

The lights were low, a fire roared in an enormous fireplace, and she heard soft symphonic music playing. Cynthia lay face down on a luxurious sheepskin area rug, wearing only underpants, as Kim sat over her, rubbing her back, wearing a see-through nightgown. *I think I know what's going on here.*

A man appeared in the doorway wearing a robe and carrying a brandy glass. It was the senator. He moved to a chair and sat, sipping his drink and watching. Cynthia raised her head, said a few words to Winthrop that Maddy couldn't understand, and sat up as Kim stood. Cynthia reached out her hands to Winthrop, who placed his glass down and walked over. He dropped his robe and was naked. He kneeled next to her, and she started kissing him. Kim came up behind him and began stroking his back.

After several minutes, Morgan and Winthrop turned to Kim, pulled at her, slipped off her nightgown, and lay her on her back. Cynthia straddled her, moved her body forward, and placed herself over the girl to receive oral sex. Winthrop penetrated Kim and began having intercourse. Maddy couldn't look on; tears welled in her eyes, overcome by old feelings of the powerful having their way with those they desired to exploit. She looked away.

After several minutes, she looked inside again, and though their positions had changed, Morgan and Winthrop still pleasured themselves with the beautiful girl. She couldn't look on, yet she was afraid to leave Kim. A loud shriek made her look back inside. Kim was on her knees, bent over the seat of a chair, and Winthrop was standing up, about to walk away from whatever painful act he'd just indulged himself in. Cynthia had already left the room.

Winthrop put on his robe, lit a cigar, and carried his glass with him as he walked out, leaving Kim lying motionless, with sweat beaded up on her back. Maddy wished she could walk in, cover the girl with a blanket, escort her to her car and take her away.

She returned to the car with her mind disturbed and indignation growing. She got in, drove to the main road, found a Howard Johnson hotel, and got a room. Lying on the bed with the lights off, her mind buzzed. *So, that man is a senator of the United States of America. He's no fucking different from Avery Jordan!* She had a powerful desire to have him brought to justice, but knew her priority was to get Kim-Ly out of Winthrop and Morgan's clutches.

After a while, her mind calmed, and she called the home answering machine. It beeped, and Adam's voice came on. "It looks like I missed you again. I wish I could talk with you about what I'm doing, but I can't. I know you'd understand." He sounded stressed, and there was fear in his voice. "I miss you and love you. I pray I see you soon."

Maddy felt Adam close yet slipping away. It shook her foundation, and she wondered why all this was happening to her again. As she lay in the lonely hotel room, hundreds of miles away from home, doubts about what she was doing started haunting her. *What if Kim doesn't want to leave? What if I'm making too many assumptions?* All felt hopeless until she heard Zep's voice saying, *Keep your head up when it needs to be up, and down when it needs to be down. Always trust your intuition.* The words gave her strength, peace came over her, and her mind grew heavy before it went blank.

When she opened her eyes, sunlight shone through the curtains, and the clock on the table read 7:55. *Shit!* She wanted to be back at the house much earlier. After a quick shower, she drove back to the dirt road and passed by the ravine with the rustic home. It was 9:33. The Mercedes was gone, but the Saab remained parked. She drove past and parked in the same place as before. She stepped through the woods toward the house, unsure of what she would do when she got there. She stopped and watched the place, hoping an opportunity would present itself.

She supposed Cynthia would leave with Kim in her car and thought she'd follow them and stay on their trail until she got the girl alone. Cynthia bolted out the front door, wrapped in a long coat, her hair pinned up. She jumped into her car and sped off down the road. There was no time to think; it was Maddy's opportunity. She ran to the house and knocked. There was no answer, so she turned the knob, and the door opened.

Kim-Ly stood looking horrified, holding a large kitchen knife. "I'm Maddy Reynolds, Kim. I'm here to get you out." The girl looked at her in disbelief.

"How do I know you are her?"

"You called me, and we spoke on the phone. You called me again, left a message, and said you feared for your life. Do you remember?"

"Yes." She relaxed her grip on the knife and let her hand fall to her side. "I called when I found out what they did to Gerald. I was desperate and looking for a miracle. But there are no miracles for people like me."

"Well, I'm here now. And I want to take you from all this."

"I can't leave. They'll just come, take me back, and it'll be worse. They told me that a thousand times."

"It's not true. You don't have to live this way." The girl looked at her with both hope and fear in her eyes.

"I want to believe you, but this is all I've known. I've gotten used to it."

Maddy thought of Stockholm syndrome. Captives develop a psychological bond with their captors during captivity. She realized she couldn't approach Kim head-on about leaving, so she asked, "Were you in love with Gerald?" She hit a nerve. The girl's face scrunched up, and tears rolled down her face. She nodded.

"He was trying to get you to leave, wasn't he?"

"I wanted to go with him, but I was too afraid." Kim reached for tissues and began wiping her face when the front door opened.

Maddy turned. Cynthia Morgan stood in the doorway, her eyes wide and face stiff, holding car keys in one hand and a carton of cigarettes in another. "I know you. You're Reynolds. You spoke at the conference at the Hilton. What are you doing here?"

"Kim needs a ride; isn't that right, Kim?" Cynthia looked at the girl, who appeared uncertain of what to do. Maddy said in a commanding voice, "Go, get your things, Kim; I'll be here waiting." The girl hesitated. Maddy repeated, "Go, Kim, get your things; there is nothing to be afraid of; I'll be with you all the way."

Kim edged to the stairs and walked out of the room. Cynthia ran to the phone, picked it up, and started dialing. Maddy walked up from behind, grabbed her wrist, and forced the phone back onto the receiver.

"You're breaking the law," Cynthia said with righteous indignation, as if the law were on her side.

"You and Winthrop have lived too long in your ivory tower, Morgan." The woman turned and tried to slap Maddy, but she grabbed her hand and shoved Cynthia against the wall. "The party's over." Kim came out while Maddy had the Senator's assistant pinned back. "Get in my car, Kim. It's up the hill; I'll be right out."

She pushed Morgan hard against the wall to make her feel pain, then added, "Were you with Winthrop the night of the masquerade party at The Glades?" Morgan didn't respond, so Maddy pushed harder. "I'm not letting you go until you answer me." The woman nodded. "Were you inside wearing a mask?" she asked, leaning harder still.

"Yes, I was there."

I knew I recognized Kim from the auction that night. "And you, the dedicated assistant to the esteemed senator. Together, you selected a sex toy that appealed to each of you; what a wonderful team you two are." It was all Maddy could do not to deck the woman before she left.

As she walked out the door, filled with disgust, she heard Morgan say, "You haven't heard the last of us, Reynolds."

It seemed to Maddy that people like Morgan and Winthrop, who violated the public trust in such a vile way, were lower than the lowest street criminals. When she returned to her car, Kim was waiting inside. She said she wished Gerald could see her now. "He'd be proud of me." She sat in her seat with her hands clenched, as if she were witnessing two cars about to collide.

Maddy spoke softly, saying there was nothing to be afraid of and she would not leave her alone. By the time they reached the interstate, Kim had sat back and seemed to relax, but when Maddy mentioned getting Aaron Purdy involved, the girl went silent. *Shit, I shouldn't have said that.* She realized Kim would need a long period of support from professionals, but what she needed most at the moment was Maddy.

She reached over and placed her hand on Kim's. "I'm sorry. We'll take things one step at a time, okay?" Kim nodded, and the tension seemed to leave her.

When she had left her place in the Adirondacks the previous day, she had no plan, only to find the girl and rescue her. Now that she'd done that, she had to handle Kim's safety and needed to develop a plan fast. "How would you like to visit with me for a while?"

Kim looked at her and said, "Sure, where do you live?"

"I live in the mountains on Berry Lake." Maddy saw fear in her eyes. "Yes, I live across from where The Glades once stood, but it's not there anymore; it burned to the ground."

Kim leaned against the door as though overwhelmed by all that was happening. Maddy asked no more questions, and Kim soon fell asleep. She kept driving north. The silence in the car gave her a chance to think through her new reality. *I don't know where this is going. This girl needs me. I can't give her everything she needs, but I can give her a sense of safety now. I'll contact Purdy tomorrow and get his thoughts on what to do next.*

She pushed her worries from her mind and let the road soothe her. When they reached the Syracuse airport she had flown out of, she turned in the rental car, hopped into her Jeep with Kim, and traveled further north until they found a diner. They ate before starting out on the last leg of the long ride to her place. Kim appeared more awake, less pensive, and she wanted to talk.

"I heard about you. Is it true you killed Sedgwick Neri?" Maddy said it was true. "We were all so afraid of him. Everyone at The Glades said he enjoyed cutting people's throats. Did he?"

"I'm afraid so."

"I wish I could have seen that place burning down. It was evil. We girls felt like cattle. The night the senator and Cynthia purchased me, I felt like an animal. It didn't take long when we got to Washington for them to, you know, start using me. I feel so..." she stopped, looked into her lap, and Maddy could tell she had tapped into a sense of shame somewhere deep inside.

"When I started as a detective, not much older than you, I collided with a man who treated children like you were. He'd have his way, then he killed them." Kim looked at her in stunned silence. "I could never understand how people like that took the road to depravity. I think it's a disease for some; others relish stealing purity from the innocent. I've battled with people like that my whole life."

The headlights lit up the empty roads, and when they passed the *Welcome to the Adirondack Park* sign, the girl lay her head back in deep thought.

The two women were quiet for the rest of the ride to Berry Lake. When they arrived at Maddy's place, it was almost midnight. Maddy got out and stretched. The cold air and lit up sky brought her back to herself. "Are you hungry, or do you need anything?" she asked Kim when they went inside.

"I'm exhausted. Just show me a bed." Maddy laughed and brought her to a spare room. Kim flopped onto the bed like a child and sighed. "Oh, this is heaven."

Maddy left her alone, went outside to the deck, and looked into the glittering sky, wondering where her life was going. There seemed to be so many puzzle pieces that didn't fit together. *First, I'm chasing the ledger, then flying to Washington to rescue a woman.* She knew she couldn't make things happen and had to let events unfold. She'd learned mysteries had a life of their own, and if you were patient, the pieces revealed themselves and formed patterns, creating a picture.

She was about to return inside when she heard a far-off, distant sound. Waiting, she heard it again; it was a howling wolf. The last time she heard it was the night of the fire, just before she found Hector dead. The painful wailing shuddered through her. She remembered how Avery Jordan had killed the wolf's mate and hung her head on his wall. She wasn't superstitious, but she believed something extraordinary would happen.

CHAPTER 16

Kim sat at the kitchen table looking across the lake when Maddy came out from her bedroom the following day. "Wow, you're an early riser."

"I'm too excited to sleep." She gazed at the panoramic view. Maddy asked if she wanted breakfast, and Kim said just tea if she had it.

As she filled a teakettle with water and fixed a pot of coffee for herself, Kim asked if The Glades had stood on that massive mountain across the lake, and Maddy said it did. "It looks so beautiful from here, but it was hell on earth for us girls imprisoned there."

"All that remains is a monument."

The girl looked at her, confused. "A monument?"

"It's reminding people of the evil we humans can do to one another."

"Hmm, I think I'd like to see that."

"Maybe we'll take a ride later. That place affected this town. People lost loved ones. They somehow feel at peace by visiting the place, knowing good prevailed."

Kim asked if she grew up in the area. "No, I grew up in Chicago and Utica."

"How did you end up in such a remote region?"

"It's a long story, and I'm afraid I'd bore you."

"No, you won't; tell me. I want to know."

Maddy looked at her as she gazed back with genuine anticipation. It was as if the girl was making up for years of confinement, trying to absorb as much as possible.

"Well, a man murdered my father when I was twelve. My dad was a detective with the Chicago PD, and I promised at his grave I'd become one too. My mom had already died, so I moved to Utica to live with my grandmother. It was just Grandma and me. I became the first woman detective in the Oneida County Sheriff's Department."

"I tracked a serial killer on my very first case. It was the beginning of several confrontations with dangerous killers. I got burned out and wanted to be as far away from city life and the craziness of the streets as possible. I had the far-out idea of moving to the mountains, and here I am. The only problem was that I built my house across the lake from The Glades. Who knew?" she said, laughing. "How about you? Where did you grow up?"

"I grew up in a small village outside Phnom Penh, Cambodia. My family was poor, with ten children. Sometimes my father would bring us to the big city. Phnom Penh is where I was taken."

She looked out the window. "I got separated from my family. A man told me he'd help me find them, and I went with him. I haven't seen them since. It's been three years, and I was eighteen. I guess I was in the wrong place at the wrong time. They think I'm dead." Maddy said maybe she'd see them again.

"Do you think so?"

"I don't see why not."

Maddy couldn't imagine what it must be like to be extracted from one's family and taken to a different country.

"Let's take a ride," Kim said.

"Sure, there's a little diner in the village. The food is pretty good, and the people are nice. We can ride up to the memorial after."

The girl asked if she could use the shower first, and when she entered the bedroom, Maddy sat, sipping her coffee, amazed at how alive the girl made her feel. She didn't realize how lonely she'd become since Adam had gone undercover.

While Kim showered, Maddy called Aaron Purdy and left a message for him to call. Later, on the drive to the village, Kim said it felt like she was on vacation. "I keep thinking I'll have to return home to Winthrop and Morgan when this is over. Isn't that silly?"

"No, it's not silly. Think of your life these last years. You've been a captive. Of course, you're going to feel that way."

Kim turned, looked out the passenger side window, and said she felt like there was a great big hole in the middle of her. "I don't even know who I am."

"Some people live an entire lifetime without knowing who they are. You're a wonderful person. Give yourself time to find that out."

The girl looked at her and thanked her. "I'm glad I have you as a friend."

They arrived at Lena's, and it wasn't too busy. Rose came over as they sat at a booth and asked who the visitor to Berry Lake was. Maddy introduced the two, and Rose sat down. "It's not busy, so I can chit-chat for a few minutes."

Kim looked at the large woman, unsure of what to make of her. "Have you told Kim about the black bear terrorizing Berry Lake?" Maddy said she had not, and Rose looked at Kim. "It's exciting; I hope I get to see it. How about the wolf? Did you hear it howling last night?" Kim said she hadn't. "Oh, there's so much to catch you up on, girl." Rose looked over her shoulder. "Oh, nuts, there's Joe; he's my boss. I've got to go, but I'll be back to take your order." When she bolted away, Kim asked if Rose was always like that. Maddy smiled and nodded, and the girl said she liked her.

Rose returned, and Kim ordered the flapjack special. "Just toast and coffee for me." Rose scooted off again, writing on her pad.

Kim hadn't made a dent in the flapjacks when she sat back. "I'm stuffed." She became quiet and seemed withdrawn. Out of the blue, she said that Gerald discovered the senator's involvement with Avery Jordan while investigating trafficking for Congressman Suarez. Maddy folded her hands and leaned over, paying close attention; the girl was ready to open up.

"Just like you, he figured out a way to meet me. He wanted to take me away from Winthrop, but I was too afraid. The more he tried, the more I fell in love with him. We'd meet at a place he rented in Northern Virginia on days I could go shopping. It was wonderful until..." she stopped, looked down, and shook her head. Maddy asked if she thought Winthrop had Gerald killed.

"I don't know for sure. If he had found out about us, he did. He's that kind of man."

"How did you know to contact me? Did Gerald give you my name?"

"No, Hector told me about you."

"Hector!" That hit Maddy hard. "How do you know Hector?"

She said she'd met him when he visited his sister at The Glades. "My room was next to Anna Jean's, and one time when he was despondent because A.J. wouldn't leave with him, he told me he was going to you for help. He said you were brave and weren't afraid of Jordan. Does Hector still live here?"

"He's the one who set The Glades on fire. Hector died that night."

Kim must have noticed the sadness in Maddy's voice. "It sounds like you were close with him."

"Yes, he was special." Not wanting to get emotional by thinking about Hector, Maddy suggested they head up to the memorial. She waved for Rose to bring the check, and soon she and the girl were on the road up the mountain. "It must have been a tremendous fire. All the large trees are gone."

"It was like hell. I thought it might spread into the town and burn it too; it was a miracle it didn't."

The girl wanted to know everything about what happened that night, and Maddy explained right up to her battle with Neri. It was the first time she'd told the entire story. The more she shared, the closer to the girl she felt; by the time they reached the top, it was like a weight had lifted. Kim gazed at her. "Wow, I did not know."

Drained from re-experiencing the drama, Maddy suggested they get out. They walked to the granite stone with the ominous words, and after reading, Kim gazed at the empty field. A breeze blew her hair back; she looked around and seemed caught up in memories. "I can still hear their voices. All those girls. I remember their faces too. They had addicted several to heroin. I wonder how many have survived."

She began walking to where the field overlooked the lake. The water shimmered with last-of-day sunlight. As she stood gazing, Kim asked, "Why is the world the way it is?" as if talking to herself. Maddy had asked herself the same question over the years and had no answer. She put her arm around Kim, and the girl laid her head on Maddy's shoulder. Together, sharing a solemn moment, it was as though they felt the spirits of those lost at The Glades gathering around. When the sun set, they walked to the Jeep without speaking.

There were no words on the drive home; they'd been transported to a place deep within themselves. As the Jeep climbed the road to the house, Maddy told her she would need to stay on the mountain for a few days for her safety. "Just until we can figure out the next steps. I have lots of puzzles and a few books you might be interested in."

"That's okay. I love Westerns, and I'm reading a good one. It will keep me busy for a while."

"Westerns?" Kim didn't seem the type to be interested in Western fiction. "What's the name of the novel?"

"*Lonesome Dove*. It has great characters." The more Maddy learned about her uniqueness, the more she liked her. When they reached the house, Kim said she was tired and went to her room. Maddy checked the message machine. Aaron Purdy had returned her call and left a number, which she called immediately.

"This is Maddy Reynolds. Much has happened since we spoke, Aaron. You said Gerald Ellis was onto something big; well, you were right. He found out Senator Winthrop had been at The Glades and purchased a young Cambodian girl as a sex slave. He and the girl fell in love as he tried to help her escape, which may have contributed to his death."

"How certain are you of this?"

"The girl's name is Kim-Ly, and she's in my house right now."

"Jesus, Maddy, she might be in danger. There'll be no witnesses if Winthrop can eliminate her."

Shit, he's right. "We need a plan to get her to a safe place."

"I can get a helicopter to your house, but it'll take a few days. In the meantime, keep the girl indoors."

"There's more, Aaron. Your team hypothesized there must be a document identifying all the participants at The Glades. There is; it's referred to as 'the ledger.' Avery Jordan kept a record of each transaction, including names."

"Where is it?"

"No one knows. It wasn't destroyed by the fire. I've been looking for it but haven't found it yet." He asked if there was anything his team could do to help find it. "No, you'll just get in the way. I'll keep trying and let you know if anything turns up. Also, Naomi White is aware it exists and is after it."

"She's bad news, Maddy."

"I'm quite aware of that, Aaron." She wanted to know what would happen to Kim-Ly when they took her.

"The FBI will place her in a witness protection program for the time being. I'll get back to you with details about the helicopter."

When she hung up, she pulled down the metal gun box from her bedroom closet shelf and lifted out the two Glocks. She loaded them, placed one in the nightstand drawer next to her bed, walked the other to her Jeep, and put it in the driver's side door panel. *Now it feels like I'm back in the shit again.*

Kim seemed at home. She found a spot to relax and read her book as Maddy walked around, checking doors and windows to ensure the place was secure. She closed the drapes, built a fire, made popcorn, and tried to act as if they were safe.

"I love this place," Kim said as she got cozy near the fireplace and put a handful of popcorn in her mouth. The firelight illuminated her face, and she looked like a little girl at a sleepover. Maddy thought of the years robbed from her. At that moment, it felt like Kim was her own child; she had a powerful desire to protect her. She asked, "What do you think you'll do when all this is over and you can live your life?"

"I don't know. I never thought about having my own life. I love nature; maybe I can find something related."

She told her about her friend Jodi, who went to the Forrest Ranger School on Berry Lake. "She now lives in Colorado and works in forest management."

Kim's eyes lit up. "Wow, how cool." Time passed, the popcorn bowl emptied, and Kim seemed at home. "Can I ask you a personal question?"

"Sure."

"Have you ever been in love?"

"Yes. I'm in love with a man named Adam."

"I never knew what it was like to feel love until Gerald. I always thought it was just about sexual pleasure. He showed me it's only a small part of it."

"You miss him, don't you?" Kim nodded and said nothing. The fire crackled, and the two sat silent until the girl said she was tired and went off to bed.

Maddy stayed by the fire, thinking about the Senator and how influential people like him behaved when threatened. *He'll use all his power to prevent exposure.*

Her thoughts drifted. *I thought depravity and violence were over after Avery Jordan killed himself, but it was not meant to be. It's still going on.* She carried her heavy thoughts to bed, and as she lay in the dark, she thought of the girl she'd saved and wondered how many more like her were still out there.

When she woke the following day, she walked to the kitchen, and Kim stood on the deck, gazing out at the snow that had fallen overnight. *Oh, my God!* Maddy thought of Purdy's warning about how people might want the girl dead. "Kim, get inside," she yelled. She ran to the window as Kim started down the stairs, cupping snow from the railing into her hand.

"Kim!" Maddy screamed when she saw movement in the leafless trees. It was a man with a rifle. He was setting up to take aim. She ran to the door, stepped onto the porch barefooted, and shouted, "Kim, get down!"

It was too late. Kim pulled her arm back, smiling, ready to throw the snowball, when a loud crack echoed through the hills. A look of disbelief riddled the girl's childlike face. A hole the size of a baseball blew through her chest, and the surrounding snow reddened. She crumpled onto the blood-soaked snow with a disbelieving expression fixed on her face; she was dead. Stunned, Maddy put her hands to her head and screamed, "No."

The guy ran down the hill, rifle in his hand. Maddy ran to her Jeep and glanced at Kim's contorted arms and legs as she passed the body. Her mouth and eyes opened with stunned incredulity, sending a thunderbolt of pain into Maddy's heart.

She jumped in the vehicle and raced down her road to Route 3. She pulled the Glock from the door panel and reached the road in time to see the man toss the rifle into the back seat of a car. He turned and fired three shots from a handgun. A round struck a tree with a pop. She got out with her weapon, took aim as he peeled out, and fired four times through his back window. The first three shattered the glass. She aimed the fourth at his head, sending the car off the road and into a tree.

Maddy moved with her gun in firing position and edged toward the guy until she saw a dark-skinned man with long hair leaning over the steering wheel. A large hole in his forehead oozed blood, and his brains were splattered on the windshield.

She kneeled on the road; her agony was too much to bear. She looked to the heavens and let loose a gut-wrenching, "Why?" A pickup rolled toward her and slowed as it approached. Johnny Johns, a local man, was inside and came to a stop. Maddy shouted for him to get the Sheriff. "Tell him there's a second body at my place." Johnny looked speechless and dumbfounded. He started for the village as she returned up the hill.

"Oh, my God," she cried as she kneeled beside Kim's body. The astonished look on the girl's face seemed to say, "What happened to my future that we talked about last night?" The expression burned into Maddy's brain. She took off her jacket and lay it over Kim's ruined face, weeping. Her pain cut deep, reopening old wounds. It felt like the night she lost her father. Her body numbed as she sat in the red snow, holding her hands over her face, weeping. Time had no meaning. The sound of a car in the driveway distracted her.

She did not move nor turn to see who it was until she felt a hand on her shoulder. She looked up, and the face of Carl Wilkins, the new young Sheriff, looked down with disbelief, searching for words.

"Call Hannah Bates at the FBI, Albany office," Maddy said, struggling to get her message out. "Tell her there's been a murder at Maddy Reynolds's home. Then come inside, and I'll tell you what happened." She stood, left the mesmerized cop alone, and walked into the house.

Like a child, she was just standing there, playing with the snow; then she was gone. Just like that, they snatched her beautiful spirit. Maddy sat holding her head, sobbing. She'd experienced many losses in the battle against the omnipresent enemy. *Now Kim is on the list.*

The phone rang, and she struggled to pick it up; it was Purdy. "I can get a helicopter to your place tomorrow morning to get the girl."

"It's too late; she's dead." After a long silence, he asked what had happened. "They were a step ahead of us. She just walked outside to play in the snow. That was all. Now she's gone."

He asked about the assassin. "I killed him, but it won't do any good to trace him to Winthrop; people for hire are always untraceable."

"I guess Winthrop wins."

"He will not win if I find the ledger."

She spent the next two hours explaining how the incident went down to Sheriff Wilkins. She didn't think the young cop had ever worked on a murder case and tried to help him understand the details and the background. She was glad the town had cleaned up the sheriff's department after all the corruption when the entire bunch was on Avery Jordan's payroll.

Wilkins said Hannah Bates had instructed him to keep the bodies in place until her team arrived. "It's hard for me to know what to say, Ms. Reynolds. This must be very difficult for you. Did you know the girl well?"

Maddy struggled to say, "She was special. She didn't deserve to die."

CHAPTER 17

Hannah

The helicopter glided over the round-top mountains to Reynolds's home. The call had come in just past noon after Hannah finished her run. Sundays were the only day she had to herself, and it always felt good to get a long jog in, then chill the rest of her weekend. But not that day.

"It's about Maddy Reynolds," Ethan had said. "We got a call. There's been a shooting at her home."

"Did they say who it was and how bad the injuries are?" she had asked.

"It's the weekend. They have translated the message a few times, and it's unclear."

"Meet me at the office; we'll take the chopper in. Also, mobilize units to Reynolds's house."

"Do you think that might be overkill, Hannah? They have a local Sherriff."

"Just do it," she barked. *Overkill,* she remembered thinking. *The kid hasn't dealt with Reynolds enough.*

Before she reached the office, she had called Ben Harris's home. His wife said he was visiting his family in Utica and wouldn't be home until evening. Hannah asked to have him call when he returned.

Endless snow-covered trees passed below as the helicopter homed in on Maddy's mountain, and an approaching expanse of water and islands signaled they were near. "When you arrive, let down behind the house;

there's plenty of room," she told the pilot. When they touched down, a young man in uniform waited, standing next to a red blotch of snow and a blue tarp over what appeared to be a body.

Hannah approached the guy. He said his name was Carl Wilkins, and he was the local sheriff. "Who's under the tarp?"

"Her name is Kim-Ly."

Aww, they killed the girl. The Suarez people had already contacted her team about Maddy taking the girl from Winthrop's assistant and that she might be his sex slave. When she told Ben Harris about it, she remembered him saying, "I wonder how many other asshole politicians are in that goddamn ledger."

"Where's Maddy Reynolds?" she asked the young sheriff. He said she was inside and added that the second body was below on Route 3.

"What second body?"

"Reynolds chased the perpetrator and killed the guy as he was trying to flee." Hannah shook her head in disbelief. She turned to an agent. "Check out the body on three."

She walked into the house and saw Maddy sitting on a sofa with her face in her hands. She moved near her. "This must have been hideous to witness." Maddy looked up, saw Hannah, and nodded.

"She was just a kid. A beautiful kid." Hannah turned to the two agents who had walked inside and gestured to leave her alone with Maddy. When they walked out, she sat next to her, unsure what to do or say, so she let the words bubble up from her gut.

"I'm sorry this is happening to you again." She thought she heard a quiet whimper, looked, and a tear fell through Maddy's fingers. Hannah placed her hand on her shoulder.

"I should have stopped her from going outside." She cleaned her face with a tissue. "All the kid wanted was to play in the snow." Hannah didn't talk her out of her self-blame; she just sat and listened. "When will this ever end, Hannah? It feels like it just goes on and on and on." She sighed, looked at Hannah with bloodshot eyes, and asked if they had told her about the other body.

"Yes, our guys are trying to identify him now." Hannah hesitated, unsure if she should bring it up, but decided she had to and added, "We heard from Aaron Purdy about the ledger." It was a lie. She hadn't heard from Aaron, but she couldn't tell her they found out by tracking her. "Once the word is out that it exists, they will come for you next."

"I know," Maddy said. An agent stepped into the kitchen and waved to Hannah to come over.

"I'll be right back, Maddy." She stepped outside. "What do you have?" she asked when she was alone with the agent.

"She killed The Snake," the agent said. Hannah looked at him and asked if he was sure. "We've got a positive ID; it's Chester Debeneau, a.k.a. The Snake." He handed over a paper.

"Jesus," Hannah said, looking at the document and then over the lake, miffed. She thanked the agent and went back inside. Maddy was washing Kim-Ly's dried blood off her hands at the kitchen sink when Hannah leaned back on the counter, watching her, and said they'd identified the guy who killed the girl. Maddy kept washing as though she was indifferent to who he was.

"He's called The Snake. He's a sought-after hitman, very expensive, and works only for high rollers, like the mob and...." Hannah didn't finish her sentence, but Maddy did.

"And politicians."

"Probably," Hannah said.

Without looking at Hannah, she wiped her hands with a towel. "You know Adam's assignment, don't you?" She kept staring at the towel, waiting for a response to the uncomfortable question. Hannah knew the woman was trying to gauge the tone of her voice to determine if she knew the answer. She answered that she did. "Is he involved in this case?" She knew the woman would see the truth, regardless of her response.

"I can't say." Maddy looked at her, smiled, and said thank you.

Hannah asked how she and Adam had been doing to lower the tension. "He's the one thing that keeps me going, but I haven't seen him in weeks."

"Stay armed, Maddy." She entered the helicopter, lost in her thoughts. As the chopper zipped over the hills back to Albany, she wondered how the drama would unfold next. She had bet on Reynolds finding her way into the heart of the mystery. That was what she had done, but they could have killed her. The stakes were higher than she wanted. She thought that leaving Maddy alone to work the puzzle would most likely result in discovering the ledger, but her survival was questionable now that she had a big target on her back.

Before she landed, Hannah got a call from Ben. He said he'd heard about the shooting at the Reynolds home and asked for the details. "The Snake killed Kim-Ly, Winthrop's sex slave. Reynolds took him out. She has already contacted the Suarez people."

"What about the ledger?"

"Maddy thinks it still exists somewhere in Berry Lake."

"Stay on it. Now that Winthrop knows he's at risk of being exposed, he'll be desperate. I need to get higher-ups involved now."

"Yes, sir." They broke off, and Hannah's mind went to Reynolds. *If I have to bet on anyone, I'll bet on her. But God forbid she doesn't make it through this; Adam will never forgive me.*

CHAPTER 18

Maddy

Each day after Kim's death felt like plodding through quicksand with a fifty-pound backpack. Maddy couldn't get the girl off her mind. Sometimes she'd sleep until late afternoon, and sometimes she'd get up before four o'clock in the morning. Then there were nights she didn't sleep at all. The only thing darker than her thoughts were the clouds that hid the sun over Berry Lake.

One morning, she brought a garbage bag to the basement and could not stuff it in a bin. She was overdue for a trip to the landfill, but wasn't up to it. "Screw it," she said. When she picked up her Stephen King book, she read a few pages and put it back down. She pulled out a puzzle from the cabinet, but her mind wasn't working right; she couldn't concentrate, and she put it back.

Naps worked, at least on some days. On other days when she tried shutting off her brain with a quick snooze, sleep wouldn't come, and she felt like jumping off a mountain. It got to where even writing in her journal was an effort. She'd start a sentence, scratch it out, and start again. Sometimes she'd forget how to spell a word. One day, trying to spell 'Wednesday,' she looked and thought it didn't seem right. She spelled it differently. After three efforts, she slammed the journal closed and threw the pen across the room. *What the fuck is going on with me?*

Each day was an eternity. She had built a wall around herself so high that even her friends couldn't scale it. Jodi left messages, but they went unreturned. The last time, she said, "I'm worried about you, Maddy. Please call me. I'm your friend, remember? There isn't anything you can't tell me. I love you, bye."

Maddy couldn't face Amber, either. Her voice quivered when she said, "Mom, why aren't you returning my calls? I want to discuss what's going on with Todd and his family. Are you okay? Please call." She also avoided Rose, fearing she'd bring her into the treachery encroaching on her world.

A single thought became so prominent in her mind that she'd spend hours ruminating over it: the look of bewilderment on Kim's face as her heart exploded through her chest. The image had burned itself into Maddy's brain. It was like watching a child being told there were no gifts on Christmas morning.

It was too much for the hardened ex-detective. Maddy had come out of the safe place on her mountain where she'd spent three years, only to have her serenity torn away and replaced with a young girl's dying eyes. She fell further into her own darkness. She didn't shower, eat well, or keep up her place.

Though she kept her weapons nearby, she did so with little vigilance. Part of her wasn't eager to fight anymore. She even wondered if it was worth it. She was losing any sense of hope, believing she drew in vicious people and that it was only a matter of time before someone made it through her defenses and took her out.

On a cloudy morning, she went to the pantry to start a pot of coffee, but the coffee can was empty. *Fuck!* She looked through the cupboards; the wine was gone, and the refrigerator had no food. *Shit! What day is today?* She looked at the calendar; it was Saturday. The grocery store in Berry Lake was closed on Sunday, so she had to push herself to go into town.

She stood before a mirror, putting on her coat. *Oh, my God.* Her hair was matted, she wore sweat clothes she'd had on for three days, and the dark circles under her eyes reminded her of a guy who'd gone fifteen rounds with Joe Frazier. *I look like a psych patient.*

She realized how far down the shit hole she'd let herself go; she wanted to die. She leaned against the wall weeping, and as if watching herself from above, she saw her life play out before her. The pain came into her from places long forgotten.

She saw herself at twelve, sitting beside her father in the ICU as he lay dying, looking foolish in a Halloween costume she'd put on just for him. They were to go trick-or-treating together. *But you never made it home. Our tradition ended with the knife Cupid thrust into your neck.*

The night in the stone quarry flashed before her. The same man returned years later to kill her, and they fought to the death in disgusting leachate from unmaintained portable toilets. *There was no relief when I escaped that misery and came to Berry Lake. No, then came young women at The Glades, who, as a sideshow in a circus, were the entertainment for evil men wanting to fulfill their lust.* Pain ripped at her guts; the ugliness she'd endured was pressing down upon her, and it was all too real. She cried out from the depths of her being, "Why me?"

Alone and feeling abandoned, she pushed herself away from the wall, dragged herself to the bathroom, undressed, and stepped into the shower. When she finished, she forced herself through the motions of combing her hair, brushing her teeth, and putting on clean clothes. She left her house and headed to town for groceries, feeling numb. The wind picked up as she carried her burdens, and a few snowflakes hung in the air as she drove.

Preoccupied as she pulled into the Tippy Top grocery store parking lot, a vehicle not typical to the area penetrated her gloom. A black BMW Coupe cruised Main Street. A man with red curly hair sat behind the wheel. *That's the guy from the airport!*

Zapped with adrenaline, her heart raced. Hannah's words popped into her head; *They'll be coming after you next.*

The car headed down Route 3 toward her house. She reached for her weapon and placed it next to her on the seat. She gave him a good head start, then followed. The guy slowed as he approached her driveway, and sure enough, he turned up her road. *I'll be damned.*

She drove halfway up, turned the vehicle, and blocked the road. *The son of a bitch will wish he hadn't gone up there because now he can't get out.* She grabbed the Glock and slid into the tall brown reeds. The snow was hard-packed, and she moved unimpeded. As she neared the end of the high grass, she stopped, remained hidden, and saw the redhead darting around inside her home.

That shithead is trashing my place trying to find the ledger, she said to herself when she heard furniture scraping her hardwood floors. His silhouette drifted toward the basement door, and she heard trash cans tossed around. After an hour, the guy walked out and got into the Beamer. He turned and started down the road; when he reached her Jeep, Maddy was waiting. He got out, holding a handgun, and started for her vehicle.

"Put it down," she shouted, hidden in the reeds. The guy turned his head in different directions, unsure where the voice was coming from. "Put it down, or I will put you down." The guy put the weapon high over his head and walked it to his car, placing it on the roof. He kept his hands high.

Maddy came out of the reeds. The guy stared at her, his face seething with anger. "Move to the front of the car and keep your hands high." He moved, but his face flushed as though embarrassed to be outsmarted. She took his weapon and slid it into the back of her pants. "Now, start walking up toward the house."

He dropped out of sight in front of the car in a flash. Maddy got low and disappeared back into the reeds, realizing he must have had a second weapon. *Shit, I should have checked.* Several minutes passed before she heard crunching snow; the guy was heading for the main road through the woods, and she followed. He halted, turned, and fired two shots about forty yards in.

Maddy didn't follow when the guy started running again; instead, she steadied herself, aimed for his leg, and fired. The redhead dropped. She ran toward him, and he started shooting from the ground. She screeched when her calf felt as if it were on fire. *Shit, I'm hit.* She stopped and fired twice more, both rounds finding their target. The guy fell backward, blood gushing from two holes near his heart.

She limped to him, ready to fire, but he lay with his eyes wide, mouth open, tongue protruding from his mouth. The man was dead.

Leaning against a tree, she shrieked, "When will this end?" The snow beneath her was red. She pulled up her pant leg, and although the wound didn't seem serious, it needed medical attention. She hobbled back to her vehicle, tied a cloth around her calf, and hoped Jason hadn't left his office. Miranda was the first to see her when she reached the town and walked into his office. "Oh, dear, what happened?"

"Is Dr. Abrams still here?"

"Come and sit," Miranda said, leading her to an examining table. "I'll get the doctor." When Jason came out, Maddy told him she had been shot. He cut her pant leg, cleaned, and scrutinized the wound. He said the bullet grazed the flesh, and it would need stitches. "I'll stitch it up and give you an injection to prevent infection, but I'll have to report it to the authorities."

Miranda assisted in the procedure, but when Jason finished, he asked if she'd leave them to speak alone. "Oh, sure," she said as she left and closed the door.

"Did this have anything to do with the ledger you told me about?"

"Yes. There are several people after it."

"I heard about the girl killed at your place. My God, Maddy, you're sure in the thick of whatever's going on. Is there anything I can do to help?"

The last thing she wanted was to get an innocent person involved and killed. "Other than letting me go through the stuff in your basement, there isn't anything. In fact, I'd like to do that tomorrow."

After a soft knock, Miranda cracked the door open. "I was going to leave for the day, but I'd be glad to take Maddy home."

"Oh, that's nice of you. But I'll be okay. Thank you, though."

When Miranda shut the door, Maddy said she would report the incident to the FBI, and they might wish to contact him. Not wanting to overwhelm Jason, she didn't tell him about the dead guy in the woods on her property.

She started for home, tired and in pain. *I haven't even gone grocery shopping, and I'm starving.* When she got to her house, she contacted Hannah Bates before attacking the mess the guy made.

"You were right. Other people are coming after me, thinking I have the ledger. One is lying dead outside my house."

"Jesus, Maddy, what happened?"

"Like you had said, another nameless face, another body. I'm using up my nine lives."

Hannah said they'd be there soon. When they hung up, Maddy limped about, putting things back in place. When the house appeared in order, she called Lena's and asked for Rose.

"I wonder if I can ask you for a favor."

"Sure, honey, what can I do?"

"First, I know I haven't been a good friend these last weeks. Since Kim died, I've been in a real rut and haven't been able to snap out."

"Oh, deary, don't fret about that; you know I'm your friend. We all have our difficulties."

"I'm in a jam. I need food, but I'm injured and can't leave my place right now. Would you bring me a cheeseburger and fries when you finish work?" Rose said, of course, and asked what happened. "I'll catch you up when I see you later."

After the call, Maddy went to her room and changed into comfortable clothes. She returned to the living room, and to keep her mind off the craziness she'd just gone through, she tweaked her stuff, trying to get things back the way they were before the guy tore the place up. She was just about finished when the rattling of a chopper shook the house.

The enormous machine landed, and as before, Hannah and three men got out. Maddy waited, and when they stepped inside, they stood around the kitchen table. "You didn't tell me about being wounded," Hannah said, aware of the police report Jason had made.

She pulled up her pant leg and said it was only a flesh wound. "I know how stubborn you are about these things, Maddy, but I think you need to let us find you a safe place until this blows over."

"We're not going through this again, are we, Hannah? I'm not running."

Hannah shook her head and changed the subject. "Where's the body?"

She explained the guy lay halfway between her house and Route 3 in the woods on the left side of her road. Hannah told two of the men to start the investigation.

"The BMW in the back of the house belongs to the guy. I had to move it because it was blocking the road. I placed one of his handguns on the dashboard."

Hannah introduced the guy at the table, taking notes. "This is Ethan Grant. He'll be helping me document what happened." The short-haired agent looked like he was still in his twenties and appeared miffed as he wrote everything down.

"I recognized the guy's red hair as he drove through the village. He was on me several months ago at the DC airport. When I saw him today, I followed him to my place and let him trash it. I waited for him to leave and confronted him, but he didn't want to be taken alive. I suppose that means he's a professional." Hannah agreed. "I'm also sure he was after the ledger."

"I don't suppose you want to tell us where you think the ledger might be."

"I do not know."

"Well, if you think of a possibility, maybe you can let us in on it. You know we'll be tearing this town apart to find it now, don't you? Ethan, do you have any more questions for Ms. Reynolds?"

"Just one. Why do you stay here when you know you're in danger?"

Maddy looked at the agent and thought how odd she must seem to him. "I would rather be dead than live in fear. I made that choice long ago."

Hannah looked at her young protégé, smirked, then turned her attention back to Maddy. "Try to keep us in the loop."

When the agents left, and Maddy was alone, she felt conspicuous. *I feel like an artifact from the old school. I guess I'm not in sync with today's law enforcement.* She knew she'd had many close calls, and she seemed foolish in the eyes of some. Yet she could not imagine living her life any other way. At moments like that, she always found comfort in thinking of her father. *I'm proud to be like you, Dad.*

It had gotten dark. Headlights lit up the trees behind the house as Rose pulled up in her station wagon. She carried a bag to the back door, and when Maddy let her in, she said she heard what had happened. "Miranda was at the diner and told everyone. Are you okay?"

"I'm much better now that you're here."

She told Rose every detail of her story between bites as she ate. Rose listened, with her elbows on the table and hands holding her head at her jaws as though not wanting to miss a word. She wept when Maddy described how it felt to kill the man trying to kill her. She pulled tissues from her purse, cleaned her face, then wrapped her arms around herself. "Dear God, Maddy, you're so brave. I can't imagine how it feels to have taken a life."

"Only God has a right to take a life," Maddy said. "I hope he forgives me when mine is over." The two moved into the living room, and when Rose sat, she noticed a book on an end table next to her.

"*Lonesome Dove.* I love this book."

"Keep it. It was Kim's; now it's yours."

Rose held it in her hand, looked up at Maddy as if realizing something, and said, "You must be in so much pain." Maddy looked away, nodded, and said nothing. Rose went to her, pulled her close, and comforted her friend.

CHAPTER 19

I need to get out of this rut. Maddy knew it was time, and she knew what to do. It was always the same; she'd force her way through whenever steamrolled by death, shock, trauma, or depression. The sun rose over the hills outside her kitchen window, and she thought about how her life felt like an endless struggle. The faces of the two men and a girl killed at her home were stuck in her head. It didn't matter if they were good guys or bad guys; they were lives lost to a sickness that brought death wherever it went.

Only God has a right to take a life, she had said to Rose, wondering if there was ever a good reason to kill someone. Maddy had taken too many and felt their weight every day. *I hope I've done the right things.*

She took her journal from a drawer, grabbed a pen, sat down, and thought before writing. *I'm revisiting a dark place within myself. I have been here before and will be here again. Life will not fool me into thinking I am helpless, have no control, or am a victim. Each day is an opportunity to make things right with the world and those I love. When I put this pen down and place this journal back in the drawer, I will leave the dark place I've dwelled and go forward with strength and hope.*

She couldn't always go deep within herself and find strength through such affirmations. During the Cupid affair, she was too young. It was her youth that allowed her to bull her way through. But when kidnapped by Jordan, she called upon her inner strength to survive.

One foot after another, she said to herself. *That's how you climb out of a hole.* She went to her room, gathered her clothes, and carted them to the washing machine. She vacuumed and dusted, then went to the drawer near the fireplace and pulled out the photo of the wolf Jodi had taken years earlier. *You've been hidden too long, my friend.* She gazed at the magnificent creature whose power had always inspired her.

Like mothers who nest before their babies, Maddy made things right with her surroundings and the people she loved before a battle. Her daughter was next; she needed to make things right with her. She nursed a cup of coffee, picked up the phone, and dialed Amber.

"Hi, honey, it's me."

"Mom? Why haven't you called me?"

"There's no good reason. I'm sorry." She explained scary things had been happening again in Berry Lake. "I was afraid of spoiling your wedding plans."

Amber's voice quivered. "You're more important than a damn wedding. And besides, we broke up," she bawled.

"Oh, sweetie, what happened?"

"We had a fight. I kept asking Todd questions like the type of invitations we should order and the gown colors. But when I asked him if he'd cut his hair for the wedding, he blew up and ran out." Maddy laughed to herself, remembering when she was in her shoes, wanting everything to be perfect. She realized how much Amber needed her.

"When did all this happen?"

"Yesterday," Amber whimpered.

"Have you spoken with each other since?"

"We talked on the phone all night." With that, Maddy knew they were in love.

"Keep talking with each other, and everything will work out fine."

"I know," Amber said, sniffling. "I told him he could grow his hair as long as he wanted. I can't believe I'd gotten so hung up on such stupid stuff."

"Don't beat yourself up, dear. We all go through it. You're learning about the things that matter in a relationship."

When Amber calmed down, she asked her mother how things were. "What's going on in Berry Lake that has you concerned?"

"There's so much that's happened. I can't explain it all. To put it simply, The Glades has reared its ugly head again. I'm in the middle of a storm. Things can become dangerous, and I want you to know how much I love you."

"Mom, you're scaring me."

"That's how it has been since you were little, right? I wish it could have been different, but I didn't choose this road; I just found myself on it. I'm afraid you're stuck with me." She heard Amber sniffle.

"I wouldn't have it any other way, Mom. And I wouldn't want anyone else for a mother. I love you too."

When she finished with Amber, Maddy got dressed and headed into town. The wind blew leaves and snowflakes across Main Street, and the village seemed abandoned. She stopped at Lena's, picked up takeout for later, then went to Jason's office. With Maynard's Chimney Service truck parked in the driveway, she pulled over in front. Someone had left the side door unlocked. She entered, and a man lay in the living room wearing blue overalls, with his head partway into the fireplace. He held a flashlight and examined the flue.

"Looks like quite a project."

Maynard looked into the room. "Either a family of squirrels moved in, or the damn thing rusted shut."

"I'll be working in the basement. I might be a while."

She switched on the basement light. The wooden stairs bent and creaked as she stepped down. *What the hell?* The basement looked ransacked; books were strewn on the floor, furniture was turned upside down, and cabinet drawers were emptied. *I know what they were looking for.*

She started shuffling through the rubble, but it was futile. Frustrated, she returned upstairs, believing someone had found the ledger. Maynard was shoving tools into the back of his truck as she walked outside, and she asked if he'd found the problem.

"You will not believe this." He pulled out a soot-covered book and handed it to her. "How in the hell do you think this got jammed up in that chimney?"

Oh my God, can it be? She grabbed a rag from his truck and rubbed the book's cover. It had green leather and a shiny crest with swirling letters that said *The Glades. It's the ledger. Hector must have hidden it there before he died.*

"I need to take this."

Maynard shrugged and told her to keep it. He got into his truck and pulled out of the driveway as Maddy stared at the precious document, holding it with both hands. The wind blew, she shivered, and Hector popped into her mind. *You want your revenge, don't you, Hector?*

A white Chevy pulled into the driveway as she was about to enter her Jeep. Miranda Southworth got out. "Hey, Maddy." She walked over. Maddy slid the ledger under the seat as Miranda approached and said she'd like to take her up on the lunch offer. "What's good for you?"

"You said Thursdays are best. How about this week?" Miranda said they were on and she'd let Rose know.

As she started driving home, she couldn't believe her luck. She wondered what had gone through Hector's mind when he hid the book. *He must have been so scared, knowing he was about to die. I wish he could have known the good in what he did. Maybe he does.*

What had started as a few snowflakes on the ride home became a squall before she reached her house. She placed the ledger atop the takeout bag she had picked up from Lena's, walked inside, wiped the book dry with a towel, and lay it on the dining room table. Now and then, she'd glanced at the holy grail as she worked in the kitchen. When she finished, she built a fire and sat with the ledger and a soft dry cloth, removing soot and grime.

Black smudges on its tungsten crest dropped her heart into her stomach, realizing it was Hector's dried blood. She cleaned the cover until the crest glittered in the firelight. Lost in wonder, it felt like the boy who had stolen it was with her.

She flipped through the pages, reading lists of names. They seemed like doomed passengers on the *Titanic*. She found where Steven Winthrop purchased a Cambodian for $450,000 on September 17, 1984. Unable to take her eyes off the entry, her indignation grew, thinking how the names and numbers were just that to Avery Jordan: names and numbers. The Cambodian was the beautiful soul, Kim-Ly. The diabolic forces involved in such debauchery were too great to comprehend.

Maddy had seen crimes of passion, power, lust, and greed on the streets. She'd seen cruel, organized crime mobsters do horrendous things to people for money and power. But this was a crime against innocence itself, the essence of all that is good in humanity. The lives of young girls were put on display before men for purchase at the altar of their lust, power, and arrogance. As she was deep in thought, the phone rang. She picked up, and it was the voice she'd longed to hear.

"It's me." A rush of emotion rose, and her eyes filled; she almost couldn't speak.

"Is it you?"

"I miss you so much. Are you well?" Maddy couldn't explain everything; she just said yes.

"How about you? Are you okay?"

"As okay as I can be without you," he said. "I can't talk, but I had to tell you I love you." She realized the call signaled he was heading into danger. She said goodbye, and she loved him too.

Frozen, she watched the fire until it faded to embers, then brought the ledger to her bedroom and lay it in the nightstand drawer next to the Glock.

CHAPTER 20

Naomi
Six weeks earlier

Find the fucking ledger, The Guy had screamed. His voice had reverberated in Naomi's head since that day. Frustrated that she hadn't made much progress with Darius Girard, she pulled out the address book again and, this time, called Hilda Heinrich.

"Hi, Hilda, it's Naomi. We need to talk, dear. Can you meet for drinks at Sammy's in the village tonight, say eight o'clock? Great, see you there."

Naomi's years running a brothel in New Orleans had brought her into contact with no-nonsense people on the darker side of the sex business. Sedgwick Neri was a brute-force killer. She had convinced Avery Jordan to hire him for The Glades's security, but Hilda Heinrich was much shadier; she even frightened Naomi.

The woman was called The Chameleon, capable of blending into almost any situation, so much so that Naomi wondered if she had multiple personalities. She could transform herself into personas and stay in a role for extended periods. Naomi had seen Hilda play the part of a debutant accompanying a foreign dignitary for weeks, acting as his mistress, and a week later, on the payroll for a drug kingpin, working the streets as a prostitute to set up a competitor for elimination.

The woman had a deep knowledge of medicines and their adverse side effects. For a while, she befriended wealthy old people, somehow becoming their beneficiaries, and when they died before their time, she collected on their life insurance policies.

When Naomi arrived at Sammy's, Hilda sat at a back table, sipping a drink from a long stem glass. "You still like them dry, I presume?" she asked Naomi as a server brought a martini she had ordered. "So, what's going on?"

Naomi explained the importance of finding the ledger. "I'm sure it's in Berry Lake somewhere. Most people who live there are bumpkins, except for one, Maddy Reynolds." She explained Maddy's background as a renowned detective who had tracked down and killed a serial killer and took out Sedgwick Neri, the throat-cutter.

Unimpressed, Hilda asked what was in the ledger. "The names of powerful people who would prefer to remain unknown." Hilda seemed to get it. She sipped her manhattan and gave Naomi a price for her services. "I see you raised your rates." Naomi gave her a cat-like stare and a smirk. "If you find the ledger, you'll get your fee plus a twenty-five percent bonus." Hilda smiled, sat back, and started asking questions.

Naomi told her it was on Avery Jordan's desk an hour before the fire. "It was not in the safe, so a kid named Hector Lemont must have taken it." She explained how he had a paper bag tucked under his arm when she shot him as he jumped from Jordan's office window. "He ran into the forest and died in an abandoned house in the village of Berry Lake."

Hilda wrote in a notebook as Naomi filled her in on the details. Naomi gave the woman a card with a phone number. "Only use this to call me. It's cellular, it's new, and the FBI can't tap it."

Three drinks later, they finished. Before departing, Naomi asked which identity she might use. "I think Miranda Southworth would fit well in this situation. She's a nurse." Hilda changed the tone of her voice, added a slight Upstate New York accent, adjusted the contours of her facial expression, and added, "I just love fall in the mountains." She winked, and Naomi shuddered. The woman gave her a smile that said, *You don't know who I am*, as she walked out of Sammy's, leaving Naomi with the tab.

CHAPTER 21

Maddy

Maddy knew the ledger was a nuclear bomb waiting to go off, and having it in her possession put her at ground zero. She dared not call Hannah Bates, fearing someone had tapped her phone. She started thinking of where to hide it. Anywhere in the house would be vulnerable to anyone who knew anything about finding hidden items. The basement seemed to require the most effort, so that's where she went.

Near the furnace and around the workbench seem too obvious, but the floor joist above might work. I'll cover it with a piece of plywood to keep it out of plain view. It will have to do for now. Using a ladder, she wedged it as best as she could up high, slipping a plywood board at an angle. "Good enough." Before leaving the basement, she noticed the trash cans were overflowing and needed a trip to the landfill. She made a mental note to go soon.

Having been cooped up for most of the previous few weeks, she wanted to get out of the house, so she headed to Lena's for dinner. When she arrived, Stick Larson got up from a booth where he sat with his friends and walked to where she was at the counter. "Hey, Maddy," the shy man mumbled. "We all heard about what happened with those guys up at your place, and, well, we're glad you're okay."

Touched by his awkward expression of concern, she thanked him. "How have you been, Stick?" He perked up and said he was seeing a new woman. "Anyone I know?"

"Miranda, Jason's new nurse."

That's odd, she thought. *Miranda and Stick seem like the most bizarre couple imaginable.* He must have picked up on her reaction and added, "She's a lot smarter than me, but she treats me real nice."

"I'm glad for you, Stick. I hope it works out."

"She's interested in Berry Lake and all its people. I showed her The Glades Memorial, and it brought back many memories. Well, I just wanted to come over and let you know we're all glad you're a part of the town, and if you need anything, just ask any of us." He headed back to the booth, where four men sat, watching him return.

Rose came over to take her order. "Miranda told me we're on for lunch on Thursday."

"Yeah, that's what we set up." She turned her attention to Stick and asked if she knew he and Miranda had become an item.

Rose shook her head. "If that isn't the strangest couple I've ever seen, I don't know what would be."

Rose took her order, and as Maddy waited, she pulled over an Albany newspaper someone had left on the counter and skimmed the headlines. On the third page, one read *Federal Probe Into Sex Trafficking Opens Investigation of The Glades.* Although the article's content revealed nothing Maddy didn't already know, she believed the blatant public announcement would further motivate all nefarious parties involved to seek the ledger.

The sun had broken out from behind the clouds when she left Lena's. Although cold, something inside moved her to the road ascending The Glades mountain. She felt the place calling her the further she went, as though she was being beckoned. She thought life went on for most people involved in The Glades's tragedy, but not for everyone, and not for her.

When she arrived at the monument, she got out, wrapped her arms around herself to keep warm, and scanned the open space. She was alone, yet she wasn't. She walked to the memorial, thinking of how it was the spot where so many sorrows had begun.

This is where Kim and all the women in the ledger lost their freedom and dignity. A breeze blew across the open field as she walked to the spot overlooking Berry Lake. Shards of light rested on the water, and the mountains looked on, seeming indifferent to the crazy woes humans had brought upon one another. She felt small standing amidst the hallmarks of time, and in their presence, she understood how her life on Earth was minuscule. *It's not how long we live; it's how well we live.*

The breeze penetrated her jacket, chilling her body. Her eyes watered and her lips were chapped. She turned back to her Jeep, and as she passed by the monument, she thought she heard a voice whispering her name in the breeze. "Maddy." She stopped and gazed at the shiny granite rock. *It's Hector.*

She closed her eyes and spoke his name; the chill left her body. She smiled, thinking of the boy whose brief life she shared for a season. She returned home feeling uplifted and pulled out her journal.

I am being prepared; I can feel it. I no longer need to understand where this guiding force comes from; I accept its presence. Will I be victorious? Will they defeat me? Will I survive? I can not answer these questions, but I can apply all my mind, heart, and soul to a cause, which is what I intend to do.

She placed the journal back into the drawer, picked up the phone, and called the person she still needed to make things right with: Jodi. When she heard the girl's sweet voice say hello, Maddy sighed, smiled, and said, "Hello, dear friend."

"Oh, Maddy, how are you?" Jodi's voice quivered. Jodi knew her friend well, perhaps better than any other. She'd stood with her when Cupid pointed a gun at Maddy's heart, and she had nudged his hand, allowing the bullet to penetrate her shoulder instead. Jodi had visited her when Maddy was stitched up in the hospital after the great fire. She had listened to Maddy question her purpose in life.

When she heard the tone of Jodi's voice, Maddy knew the girl understood she was facing death again.

"You've been on my mind, night and day. How bad have things gotten?"

"Let's just say I'm calling to tell you how I've been in a downward spiral, unable to speak with my best friend, and I want you to know how sorry I am." Maddy couldn't discuss the ledger or share all that had happened, but she knew Jodi would sense the situation and not press for more information.

"What about now? What are you going to do?"

"I'm not afraid. I'm prepared for whatever might be. I want you to know how grateful I am for your friendship."

Maddy heard Jodi weeping before saying, "And I for yours." It was as though they both knew any more words would detract from the moment; both hung up without another word.

CHAPTER 22

It was Thursday, and Maddy was to have Rose and Miranda over for lunch. She checked the refrigerator and decided she needed to make a grocery store trip. Although she wasn't up for a gathering, she thought being with a few friends might help her come out of herself. She got dressed and headed to the village.

Stick Larson walked in her direction as she rolled her cart through the aisles of Tippy Top Grocery Store. She thought he didn't look well, and when he approached and stopped, he moved his head from side to side, avoiding eye contact. He reached her and said hello.

"Hi, Stick. Are you okay?"

"Well, not really." He seemed reluctant to elaborate, and Maddy didn't want to push him, but he added, "I suppose I can tell you since I told you about Miranda and me. We broke up, or maybe 'she broke up with me' is a better way to put it."

Maddy could see he was holding back tears and said she was sorry. He grimaced and told her he just couldn't figure it out. "She had been so nice to me, but the other day when I sat next to her at Lena's, she got up without saying a word and moved to a different booth. I tried talking to her as she left the diner, and she told me to leave her alone. I do not know what I did wrong."

Maddy felt terrible for the guy. She had thought the relationship wasn't a good fit when she realized they were dating, but now it seemed apparent the woman was using the naïve man. "You didn't do anything wrong, Stick. Some women are fickle."

"I suppose," he said, nodding before moving on to check out. The incident caused Maddy to think Miranda's insensitivity toward Stick revealed a not-very-admirable quality about the woman.

As she drove home, a black streak of dark gray clouds looked painted by a giant brush across the eastern sky. It had moved halfway across the heavens by the time she reached her place. She changed, cooked, and got everything ready, just as Rose and Miranda pulled up in Rose's station wagon. Each woman held an item they carried to the back door.

"Oh, hi," Rose said, smiling, excited to have a gathering with friends. "I made an apple pie." She set it on the counter.

Miranda said she bought ice cream to go with the pie. She pulled away when Maddy tried to take the vanilla bean and put it in the freezer.

"Oh, that's okay; I'll take care of it." Miranda went to the refrigerator, opened the doors, and looked around before putting the ice cream inside the freezer. *That's odd*, Maddy thought.

"Why don't we sit by the fire for a while before eating?" she suggested. They went to the living room and got comfortable. Rose explained how she just had snow tires installed that morning because a massive storm was supposed to be heading their way.

Maddy mentioned how she noticed the sky turning black earlier. "It must be a nor'easter. We haven't had one in a few years.

"How much snow do you get when a storm is like that?" Miranda asked.

Rose told her three years ago, they got four feet. "No one left their houses for a week." As she and Miranda chatted about the snow, Maddy's mind went to the filled-up garbage cans in her basement that needed to be taken to the landfill. *If I get snowed in, they'll overflow before I can get there.*

As the conversation drifted to the kitchen, Maddy noticed Miranda gazing at the refrigerator as though there was something she needed to do.

She wondered what was with her. When Maddy brought out fish, beef, and chicken tacos with the fixings, she set the plates on the table and said, "Let's sit."

"Isn't this delightful?" Rose eyeballed the savory meal before her. They sat down, and the conversation got around to Stick Larson. It was as though Rose couldn't help herself from inquiring about what had happened between Miranda and him.

Miranda rolled her eyes and huffed. "When I first came here, I was kind of lonely. Stick was fun for a while, but I'm not interested in farm tractors and automobile engines. I guess we're just not a good fit." Maddy noticed Rose's eyes fixed on the woman as though she wanted to say something, but she held her tongue because it wouldn't have been nice.

When the coffee was ready after they ate, Maddy went to the cupboard and returned with three cups and saucers. Rose got up to cut the pie. "I'll get the cream for the coffee," Miranda said and went to the refrigerator. "You take yours black, don't you, Rose?" When Rose nodded, Miranda asked Maddy, "You take cream, right?" Maddy said she did. She brought the creamer to the table, and Rose carried a dish with pieces of pie.

Maddy poured cream into her coffee and handed the creamer to Miranda. "Oh, no, I take it black." Maddy's mind snapped to the first time she met the woman in Lena's, and she had asked Rose to bring her cream for her coffee. *What gives with her?*

As she often did, Rose told one funny story after another, and Maddy's stomach hurt from laughing so hard. *It feels so good to let loose with her.*

"Oh, look." Rose took a break from her comedy routine and gazed outside. The snow was falling hard. She turned to Miranda and said they should go or they might not make it to the village, snow tires or not. They stood. Miranda and Rose put on their coats, and everyone moved toward the door. "That was great fun," Rose said.

"Yes, thank you, Maddy. I enjoyed myself." Miranda smiled.

The two women went outdoors and got into the car, and Maddy watched them fade into the falling snow. She noticed a swath in the snow along the side of her house. *That bear is coming around. I've got to make a trip to the landfill.*

She sighed, relieved the gathering was over, but she had to admit, she had fun. *How can you not when you're with Rose?* She looked at the dirty dishes piled in the sink, felt a wave of fatigue, and let them sit. *I just feel like lying down,* she thought. She went to the sofa, covered herself with a throw blanket, and fell into a deep sleep.

She woke up in a strange dream. Her surroundings appeared blurred; she was still in her living room but semiconscious. *Am I awake or dreaming?* She tried to stand, but couldn't move. Her heart throbbed; she heard it pounding against her chest. Struggling to move, she tried waking herself, but couldn't budge. The dream differed from any she'd ever had. She lay frozen. Although she could see the surrounding room, it was fuzzy, and she could only slightly move her eyes.

When she had come out of anesthesia after her surgery, she had felt similar, but nurses were around to calm her and let her know she would be alright. She tried screaming, hoping it would pull her out of the sleep stupor, but the words got stuck in her throat.

Her heart pounded harder. Warmth around her neck and face grew hotter. Sweat dripped into her eyes, and they burned. She heard a sound, felt cool air, and realized the back door had opened. She heard footsteps in the kitchen, glimpsed an unrecognizable image moving around, and tried to say, *I'm out here!* But no sound came out. *This is not a dream; I've been drugged.*

The image in the kitchen moved around as though it knew what it was doing. Maddy heard something plop onto the kitchen table, and the figure opened what appeared to be a satchel or a bag. *What the hell is going on?* It turned and moved toward her, holding something small. It was a woman, and when she got closer, she put her face right up to Maddy's. *It's fucking Miranda! I knew she took cream in her coffee.*

"Hi, dear." Miranda smiled, speaking the way a mother might talk to a toddler. "Are you not feeling well, honey?" The woman's face filled Maddy's field of vision, and each time she turned her head, it appeared to change shape. Miranda's distorted, perverse, drug-affected image made her look like Quasimodo from *The Hunchback of Notre Dame.*

She used all her strength to move her limbs, but they would not obey. *I'm trapped in my body!* She could see Miranda moving about her place, but with limited ability to turn her eyes, she moved in and out of her field of vision. *What the hell is she doing?*

She held a syringe close. "This is Aunt Miranda's special sauce; it will make us great friends. But first, we must make you nice and comfy."

She set the syringe on the end table. Maddy felt her body turn to lay on her back. Her feet stretched straight, her head lifted, and Miranda shoved a pillow beneath. "This might take a little while, so I want you to feel relaxed."

I never thought of what it would be like to be an invalid; I'd rather be dead. Saliva dripped down her face, and Miranda dabbed the moisture with a tissue. "Oh, I can see you're eager for my special sauce; just be patient; it's coming." She lifted the syringe, flicked the needle a few times, and Maddy felt a light prick.

"That wasn't so bad, was it? Aunt Miranda is very good at doing this. I'll let you rest a while; I have things to do. If you need anything, just holler. Oops," she chuckled, "I forgot, you can't."

Maddy's mind was heavy, her thoughts mushy; one was running into another. The surrounding objects took on a strange glow, and she knew she was under the influence of a powerful drug. *My will is about to be tested. I hope I can withstand this. Miranda wants the damn ledger and will stop at nothing to get it.* She fell into a murky sleep.

Like she was swimming in mud, she struggled to breathe. An earthy ammonia odor grew strong, and she realized clumps of moist dirt were being shoveled upon her. *I'm in my grave,* she wailed as fear riveted her body.

She looked around, and blackness was everywhere. There was no glimmer of light, no sign of relief, no one to rescue her. Never had she felt as doomed as in that moment. She was about to descend into hopelessness when a hand jostled her out of the dream. "Good morning. I hope you slept well last night. Time to rise and shine."

Miranda's sickly sweet tone gave Maddy a powerful urge to kick out the woman's teeth. She lifted her leg to get up, and although she was no longer paralyzed, she was tied down and couldn't move.

The room was bright. Light streamed in the windows, and Miranda went to the chair across from her. When she tried to say, "What are you doing?" her words slurred.

"I should tell you, the special sauce makes your mind fuzzy and causes you to talk like you're drunk, but it will help you tell the truth. I tell all my clients, or maybe I should say my *victims*, this can be as easy or as difficult as you make it; it's up to you. Now, I know you have the ledger, so why not save yourself all the painful things I plan on doing and tell me where it is?"

Maddy tried to say, 'I don't have it,' but it came out, "Iyounit."

Miranda threw her head back, laughing. "You sound so silly; now let's try that again. Where is the ledger?" Again, the words garbled together. "Let's do this differently; shake or nod your head to my questions. Can you hear me?" Maddy nodded. "Very good. Are you Maddy Reynolds?" Maddy nodded again. "We're doing so well. Now, do you have the ledger?" She shook her head. "Oh, no. I think you want to make this difficult on yourself."

The woman got up, stood over Maddy, and pushed her thumb into her right lower neck, sending intense pain to her right temple; she screamed. "That should loosen your memory. Now, do you have the ledger?" Again, Maddy shook her head. Miranda buried her thumb into the left side of her lower neck.

The pain traveled to Maddy's forehead; she squinted her eyes and screamed, "Bitch!" Her head throbbed. It felt like powerful men were twisting on each end of every nerve between her ears until they were about to snap. Miranda smiled, pleased with the power she held and her talent for inflicting pain.

Maddy began talking to herself, cajoling and encouraging her inner being to stay strong. *You can do this, Maddy. Hang in there.* Tears rolled down her cheek, and she felt like she was about to vomit.

"One more time now. Do you have the ledger?" She shook her head. Miranda stood over her, placed both thumbs on the pain points, and dropped her entire body weight. Maddy twisted, turned her head from side to side, vomited, and gagged. "Oh, what a mess." Miranda stepped back as sweat soaked through Maddy's clothes while she gasped, trying to clear vomit from her throat and nose.

"Well, we'll have to let you lay in your mess for a while before we start session two. You shouldn't have had the fish tacos yesterday; they smell nasty when they're regurgitated. And by the way, I've got plenty of time. It's snowing so hard that I'd never make it out. I'm sure glad I brought plenty of food." The woman disappeared out of view as Maddy lay breathing heavily, in pain, and feeling sick.

She forced her mind to a dreamy place, thinking of people she loved: Amber, Jodi, Rose, Adam, and her father. Pretending they were with her, witnessing her misery and encouraging her with their love helped strengthen her. Then her mind went to the woman torturing her, and she remembered being on death's doorstep with Cupid and Neri. She told herself she wouldn't let that bitch Miranda break her.

Maddy tried focusing on what she had to do to survive, but the stench of vomit, made worse by leftover food reeking in the kitchen garbage bin, roiled her stomach and distracted her, making it hard to think. Then she thought, *The bear!* The stinking garbage might attract the ravaging animal. She knew the basement bins were full. They were rank, and the bear had been checking out her place. *I need to get that rotting food from the kitchen into the basement.*

When Miranda returned, she said, "I'm going to let you think a while, dear, because what I have in store for you next makes what I've done so far pale."

"I can't think at all," she yelled. "It stinks in here!"

"Yes, the rotting fish tacos in the kitchen smell worse than your vomit."

"Toss the damn bag into the basement," Maddy shouted.

"I believe that's a good idea," Miranda said. She went to the kitchen and carried the bag from the bin to the basement door; it hit the concrete floor with a clank.

It was getting dark. Miranda looked out the window. "It looks like I will be here a while; that snow just won't stop. I believe I'll use your bed to rest awhile; we'll resume our fun later."

Maddy fell into a haze, thinking of her life. She wished she had spent more time with her daughter. *She needs me. I've always been so absorbed in my problems; I wish I'd done things differently.* When she realized she might not make it, regrets poured into her head. *If I make it out of this, things will be different.*

It startled her when she felt Miranda unbuttoning her shirt. "Good morning, dear. It's time to begin session two. I was hoping I wouldn't have to do this, but you're not giving me any choice." The woman clamped electric probes to the skin above Maddy's left and right clavicles and wired each to a black box containing a rheostat. Another wire went from the box to the wall plug.

Miranda explained the rheostat controlled the electricity going into Maddy's body. "This device goes up to twenty, but we'll begin at level five. Before we start, I think a little more sauce is in order."

Maddy lay helpless as Miranda prepared the syringe, dreading what she was about to endure. She felt intense pressure in her bladder; she needed to urinate. Again, a pinprick and her thoughts went sloshy.

The depraved woman stood over her, holding the black box, and asked if she had the ledger. This time, Maddy screamed, "No!"

"Okay, here comes number five." She flipped the switch. Electricity zapped Maddy's upper torso and head, and fireworks exploded in her brain. Dazed, she couldn't think; her tongue numbed, her heart raced, and she couldn't speak.

"That number five is nasty, isn't it?" She sat with her legs crossed, sipping a cup of coffee as if watching a movie. She added, "I saw skin melt once." Maddy's stomach churned, listening to the woman's perversity. "Of course," Miranda continued, "the person was fairer complexioned than you, but the smell of flesh burning is something to behold, I tell you."

"Where was I? Oh, yes, I was asking you about the ledger. Do you have it, dear?" Maddy shook her head. "Oh, my, we'll have to go to number ten."

The zap was so powerful that Maddy convulsed, her body rattled, and her bladder emptied. Staring at the ceiling, unable to think or speak, she heard Miranda say, "Oops, that may have been a little too much." Miranda giggled. "Oh dear, it looks like you went potty. That reminds me, I have to go too. I'll be right back."

Maddy lay in agony, trying to numb her body to the pain. She couldn't stop thinking of the intense burning in her chest. She'd endured the pain of two gunshot wounds and her flesh sliced with a razor-sharp knife, but nothing hurt as much as high voltage electricity running through her skin.

The drug had a powerful sedative effect, and she began fading into blackness, but a crash snapped her out of it. *What was that? Was that in my dream? Did it come from the basement?* She thought she heard rustling. She lay above the trash cans' location. She wasn't sure if it was the bear, but realized she couldn't survive another electric shock to her brain and had to do something. *Come on, Mr. Bear, make it be you.* A bottle broke in the basement, and a tin can struck the concrete floor. *It's got to be him.*

The toilet flushed, and Maddy had to decide what to do. When Miranda returned, she said, "Now, are we ready to try number fifteen?" She picked up the black box and looked like she was about to flip the switch when Maddy shouted, "No more; I have the ledger." A self-satisfied smile grew across Miranda's face. It seemed to say, *I've broken the great Maddy Reynolds.*

"It's in the basement." She huffed with exasperation. She knew if the bear wasn't there, Miranda would return and try to kill her. Miranda asked where in the basement it was. "I'll have to show you."

"Oh, no, you don't. I've heard about your tricks. You tell me where it is, and I'll find it. And in case you have any ideas of getting your handgun, it's right here." She held up the Glock from the nightstand. "So, where in the basement is it?"

"It's hidden behind the workbench."

"It better be. If I come upstairs without it, you'll get level twenty." She pointed the gun at her, cut the plastic tie binding Maddy's feet, and told her to stand up. "I want you near me. I'm not letting you pull a rabbit out of your hat. And remember, I know how to use a pistol." She helped her to her feet.

"I'll follow you to the basement door." Miranda walked behind as Maddy struggled on wobbly legs to a door off the kitchen. She opened up. "I want you on your knees with your back to the stairway, so I can see you when I go down. And believe me, I have no qualms about shooting someone in the back."

She flipped on the light and walked down a few steps. "Now kneel and turn your back to the stairs." A shuffling sound came from the basement and Maddy glanced over her shoulder. Miranda was looking downstairs, trying to see what it was. Like a mule, Maddy thrust her right leg and kicked Miranda, sending her tumbling. She crawled forward and, using her back, pushed the door shut, then turned the lock with her lips. She moved to the side, away from the door.

A gunshot was followed by a deafening roar. Miranda began screaming, "You fucking bitch! Let me out of here!" Loud shuffling on the stairs sounded like she was trying to climb to the door. She howled, "Let me out of here, please!" She started scratching at the door. Several loud thumps followed, and Maddy realized the bear was dragging her back down the stairs.

A cacophony of ear-piercing yelps followed intermittently, begging. "Help me, please help me! Ahhh, help me! You fucking bitch! Help me!" Gut-wrenching whaling and several agonizing minutes of Miranda's pitiful howling ended with a final, high-pitched squeal, like a pig being slaughtered. Then silence.

Maddy heard something she couldn't identify. It grew louder. Then she recognized the chomping and grunting sounds of the bear eating Miranda. She sat on the floor, listening to the beast devour the woman. With the sickening sounds of human flesh being torn, bones crushed, and poison rotting in her gut, she leaned over into a ball of agony.

Her brain was fried, and her intestines felt like Drano was eating at her abdomen; she tried not to move. She lay, allowing oxygen to reenter her blood, pushing out the special sauce toxins still percolating in her body.

With her hands still bound, she used the wall to work her way to a standing position. She shuffled to the fireplace and used the rough stone hearth to break the plastic ties around her wrists. She tried to walk but stumbled around, holding onto the wall to keep from falling.

She steadied herself and made her way to a window overlooking the back. The monster black bear dragged Miranda's body toward the woods, leaving a trail of blood in the snow. It stopped every twenty yards and shook the rag doll-like figure as its head and limbs flopped around. One leg was eaten off.

Maddy made her way to her room and collapsed onto the bed. Moaning, she wanted to die. It was as though Miranda had run her body through a meat grinder, and now it was an open abscess. Her heart pounded for several minutes, and she worried she might have a heart attack. She started to sustain steady breathing and fell asleep.

CHAPTER 23

Naomi

Naomi hadn't heard from Hilda Heinrich, The Chameleon, for two weeks. The last she knew, the woman was playing the role of a nurse named Miranda Southworth. The lack of information stressed her, and her occasional emergency cigarette had become a two-pack-a-day habit. She'd grown so tense that she canceled her regular rendezvous with Drake.

The Chameleon had left a message saying, "You put me onto that Stick character, and what a trip he is. I had to throw myself at him to meet me for coffee in that greasy spoon, Lena's. He told me Hector had a cave in the woods where he stayed before the fire, so I got him to take me for a hike. We stopped at the wretched hole in the ground, and aside from a few rusted pots and pans, all I found was a mildewed, mice-infested sleeping bag."

The woman also said she thought Reynolds might have found the ledger. "I have lunch at her place soon with fat Rose." Naomi had warned her to be careful with the ex-detective, but The Chameleon told her to chill out and not worry about it; she could handle her.

Naomi hadn't told her she'd gotten another call from The Guy and what he said. He had known about Reynolds taking the Cambodian girl and worried she could expose Senator Winthrop. "You cannot allow that to happen," he had screamed, insinuating Maddy had to be killed. He also wanted The Chameleon dead.

She was making herself crazy, sitting around her flat, smoking cigarettes, and waiting to hear from Hilda, so she changed tactics. She had to play her cards right, one hand at a time, and now that The Guy insisted Reynolds and The Chameleon must go, it was time to become proactive.

Despite her disdain for being in the mountains, she started contacting realtors in the Central Adirondacks, looking for a rental from where to operate until she settled things. After a few hours on the phone, she rented a place on Star Lake, eleven miles from Berry Lake.

She packed her bag with warm clothes, left her place, and rented a four-wheel-drive vehicle. She arrived at the rental the next day, late in the afternoon. Not used to cooking for herself, she brought several bags of groceries, hoping she had what she needed for an extended period. She parked in a rutted, frozen driveway, walked onto the porch of what appeared to be a grand Adirondack camp, and stepped into a vast living room with glossy hardwood floors. It had a fireplace and large windows in the back that overlooked the frozen lake.

Surprised at the splendor of the massive house, after unloading the vehicle, she perused the place and found its furnishings of good quality and very comfortable. Since it was off season, no neighbors were around, which suited Naomi fine. As far as she was concerned, it was as good as thirty floors above street level.

Her biggest surprise was that they had hooked the place up to cable television. Aside from the windows rattling when the wind blew off the lake, she was comfortable and felt safe as long as she kept her Colt snub-nosed revolver nearby.

With the fireplace roaring, she relaxed, and on her third manhattan, she started flipping channels on the TV. She stopped when she saw Herman Suarez talking on CNN. "Although I can't say much about an ongoing investigation, I can say we are confident we will bring several participants of sex trafficking to justice. Many are notable figures." She knew what that meant. It meant the government was also hot on the trail of the ledger.

Anxious again, she wished she hadn't turned on the television. She paced around, holding a cigarette, and when she glanced out the back window, she couldn't see the lights across the lake. *What the hell?* She flipped on the backyard light, and snow swirled so thick she couldn't see the picnic table in the yard, visible only an hour earlier.

She felt helpless and needed to regain control. She went to her purse, dug out the cellular phone, and dialed Darius Girard. Not expecting anything had changed since she saw him in San Antonio, she called as much to release her nervous energy as for any other reason.

A woman answered, and when she asked for Darius, she said she'd get him. He wanted to know who it was, and Naomi said to tell him it was an old friend from The Glades. Darius took the phone. He spoke in a loud whisper, "Don't ever say The Glades when you call me, Naomi. No one here knows about that."

It was a mistake to allow Naomi to know one's sensitivities, for she loved to use them to put herself into a position of power. "I told you before that you can't run from your past. I just thought I'd call to see if anyone has contacted you since we last spoke." She expected him to say no, but when he told her Maddy Reynolds had been to see him, she lost it. "Maddy Reynolds! Paid you a visit!" She stood and had to work at not throwing a shoe through the picture window. "What did she want, Darius?" she screamed.

"Among other things, she wanted to know if you had been to see me."

"What?! You didn't tell her, did you?"

"Why, yes, I did." He seemed to enjoy being in control for a change.

She raged, bit her lip, ran to her cigarettes, and lit up. She started pacing the wooden floors again. "You said, 'Among other things.' What other things?"

"For the most part, she was following up on a murdered congressional aide."

"Quit playing fucking games with me, Darius. What do you mean, 'For the most part?' What else did she want to know? Tell me everything."

"You mean, did she know about the ledger?" He seemed amused.

"Yes. Does Reynolds know about the ledger?" Naomi knew Darius acted that way because he felt safe two thousand miles away. If he were in the same room as her, things would be different because he'd know she'd gouge his eyes out if he were to act that way in her presence.

"Yes, she knows."

"I can't believe you told her about the ledger."

Girard said he didn't tell her; she knew. Naomi realized even if he had told Reynolds, Darius was astute enough not to admit it because the long arm of the mob reached well into San Antonio.

"I don't have to tell you what will happen if I drop a dime on you, do I?" Darius went silent, as though thinking he had pushed her too far. He asked if there was more, and Naomi said, "Only that I expect you to call me if anyone makes inquiries." She threw the phone onto the sofa and crossed her arms, feeling more helpless than before.

I wish The Chameleon would call me. The woman worked independently and wouldn't allow anyone to look over her shoulder or second guess what she did. Naomi knew that when she hired her. It was part of the deal, but she knew she had put too many eggs in Hilda's basket and might need to develop Plan B.

CHAPTER 24

Hannah

It was Friday afternoon when the snowstorm made its way into Albany. Hannah watched from her office window as a wall of white blocked her view of the parking lot. It was 4:30, and she last spoke to Ethan at about noon. He had told her the storm was swooping down more from the north than the east and was pounding the Central Adirondacks.

She shoved papers into her briefcase before leaving the office for a retirement gathering for one of her agents. Marty Capria had maxed out at the FBI-mandated retirement age after twenty-five years of service. He was an excellent agent and a likable character, and Hannah knew there'd be a crowd at Fennel's Bistro, snowstorm or not.

She zipped her shoulder bag, grabbed her cellular phone, and asked to be updated with any developments on the trafficking case. She plodded her way through the snow in the parking lot to her car and headed to Fennell's. The place was about five minutes from the office in typical weather, but her Audi bogged down in slow-moving traffic, and after twenty minutes, she was only halfway to the restaurant.

The phone rang, and it was Ethan. He was working an off shift to cover the case and said he had an update. "It looks like electricity and phone service are out around Berry Lake, and we can't track Reynolds."

"Shit." She was frustrated as her car sloshed through the wet snow. "I'm headed to Fennell's for Marty's party; keep me posted." She felt the tension rising to the spot around her temples, a sensation that sometimes telegraphed a migraine. *I can just hear Ben now,* she thought, thinking of her boss's reaction to losing contact with Reynolds.

She walked into the bistro with a face full of snow. The ruckus in the back room led her to where people sat laughing, with several pitchers of beer scattered around a long table. Marty sat at the center, looking lit up like a Christmas tree. *I sure hope somebody's driving him home,* she thought.

Hannah sat near the end of the table and tried to smile as the traditional ceremony of presenting gag gifts was being conducted. She never enjoyed boisterous beer-for-alls, but she loved the people around her and gave it her best, although her mind was on Reynolds.

Ten minutes after she arrived, Ben Harris walked in and sat next to her. Although he didn't say anything about work, she knew he was as concerned about the situation as she was. When Marty opened a wrapped gift box with a pack of condoms inside and a note that said he didn't need to hide fucking off anymore, Hannah heard the phone ring in her purse over the roar of laughter. She left the table and walked to a quiet area in the next room.

Ethan gave her an update, and the tension around her temples became twisting pain. When she returned to the table, Ben asked what was happening. In a soft voice, so no one else could hear, she told him the storm knocked out power and phones around Berry Lake. "We don't know what's happening with Reynolds."

Ben nodded, and she continued. "We also haven't had any sign of Naomi White." Hannah noticed Ben's expression sour, like he'd bit into a juicy lemon. "She hasn't used her phone for several days, and when we sent someone to her Manhattan place to check it out, they were told she left town three days ago and hasn't been back."

"So, you've lost her."

"It looks like it."

"Is there anything more?" *Now the hard part,* Hannah thought to herself.

"It looks like White hired Hilda Heinrich."

"Jesus!" Ben said it loud enough for a few partiers to look over. He caught himself and lowered his voice to a whisper. "Hannah, she's killed more people than the fucking plague." He calmed himself and added, "So, let me get this straight. You don't have eyes on Reynolds because of the storm. Naomi White has disappeared, and Heinrich, the Goddess of Death, is doing her shtick somewhere in Berry Lake. Is that about right?"

"I think you nailed it, Ben," Hannah said, looking down at the table. He wasn't the type to micromanage or panic, but he wasn't the kind to put perfume on a pig, either. Straight-faced, Ben insisted they needed to reestablish contact with Reynolds ASAP, set up a command center near Berry Lake, and have a unit ready to move in at a moment's notice. Then he added, "And pray to God there are enough people left alive in Berry Lake to tell us what ends up happening." He finished his drink, congratulated Marty on his retirement, and left the bar.

That went well. She had already set everything Ben suggested in motion, but knew better than to tell her boss while pissed off. She hung out at the party for about an hour before saying goodbye to Marty and headed out into the falling snow.

No sooner than she started her car, the phone rang, and her counterpart with the New York State Police, who worked on the case in tandem with her team, was on the line. He said they heard from their man on the inside that the mob's muscle team was in place and about to make their move. She realized that meant that Adam had moved into harm's way. The tension in her temples turned into a full-blown migraine.

When she arrived home, the house was empty, and she was relieved her husband and son were at a basketball game. Sometimes explaining why she had to do things, like leaving in the morning for an unknown period, required more mind-share than she had, especially when her head felt like it was about to explode.

She needed a good night's sleep and would talk to them about what she had to do over breakfast. Before going into bed, she took medication for the migraine so it wouldn't paralyze her and began packing a duffel bag with clothes she hoped would keep her warm in the near-zero Tupper Lake weather. The place was thirty-five miles from Berry Lake, where the new command center would be set up when the storm relented.

Saturday morning at the Bates home was a time for relaxing before everyone went off to do their own thing. Hannah walked into the kitchen, and Anthony, her husband, sat with his head buried in a newspaper. Her son Charles checked game scores in the sports section. She poured her coffee and sat between them, trying to decide how to explain she'd be leaving in an hour for a place she couldn't reveal and for a period that she didn't know.

"So, how was the game last night, boys?" She hoped they'd peek over their newspapers. Anthony looked over his reading glasses and told her not to try hiding her little secret; they knew she was about to abandon them again. She knew his smile was to telegraph he wasn't angry and only that he was on to her.

"How did you know?"

"Leaving the gun cabinet ajar, where you keep your extra weapon, was a dead giveaway." He smirked, as if to say she should know better. "Maybe you wanted us to know." Anthony was a psychiatrist and always looked for Freudian meanings behind people's words and actions.

"Can it, Sigmund," Hannah quipped back, relieved that he wasn't upset. Charles's head remained buried in his paper as his parents spoke.

"Don't tell me. You can't tell us where you're going, and you don't know how long you'll be gone," Anthony added. "But wherever it is, it must be mighty cold because I saw your thermal mittens and snow boots were missing from the closet when I went to grab the snow shovel this morning."

"You should do my job." She placed her hand on his forearm; he kissed it and sighed. His eyes said, *I'm going to miss you.*

As always, sadness weighed on Hannah's heart whenever she left her family. She finished her coffee, stood, and kissed Anthony on the forehead. Her son piped up. "Hey, what about me?" She smiled, walked over, and put her arms around his head. Cuddling him to her breast, she kissed his forehead.

After she finished packing and gathering her stuff, she headed to the office where she was to meet Ethan and others on her team. She wondered how circumstances might have changed during the information blackout in Berry Lake. She knew Maddy had to be the target for anyone looking for the ledger, and the storm might work to the advantage of perpetrators planted around her. She hated losing control of a case, especially when using an innocent the way the FBI used Maddy. She wondered if she should have intervened and tried extricating Reynolds sooner.

Ethan waited at the office, and when she arrived, he said the helicopter was ready. "The weather forecast shows the snow is abating in the Central Adirondacks. It will take us about ninety minutes to get to the command center location, so we can leave any time now."

He gave her an update when they were in the air and heading north. Little had changed, except Adam Forsyth had penetrated the muscle team. *Maddy and Adam are entering a death zone together,* she thought, wondering how the ordeal would play out.

CHAPTER 25

Maddy

Maddy rolled over in bed as she emerged from a dark and dreamy place. She knew she was in her bedroom, but not much more. Recollections of what Miranda had done dribbled into her mind as every nerve in her neck and head screamed. *I have to move my body.* She forced herself to a sitting position. Her stomach churned as if she'd eaten rancid meat, and her chest felt like someone had used it for an ironing board. Pushing herself off the bed, the memory of Miranda's torture returned.

Disorientated, she walked into the bathroom and saw herself in the mirror. "Oh, dear Lord!" Her face was drooping, her eyes sunken in, and her hair stuck together with vomit. She leaned on the counter and wanted to collapse. She took heavy deep breaths, pushed herself to take off her clothes, and ran the shower water. As she waited for the water to warm, she tried moving her bowels but couldn't. *What did she put into my system?* She thought of Miranda's special sauce.

She stepped into the running water and felt it cleanse the reeking stink from her body. She wept. Weakened, wondering how much more she could take, she wanted it all to be over. *What do you want to do, Maddy? No! You cannot give up. You must keep living.*

The water grew cold, and the pressure weakened. *Oh, shit! I know what this means.* She stepped onto the freezing floor and realized the electricity was out. *Oh, no.* She threw her head back, closed her eyes, and wanted to scream.

Push yourself, Maddy, she heard herself say. Although exhausted, she searched the closet's darkness and found sweatpants, wool socks, and a heavy sweater. She huffed as she put them on and could see her breath.

She went to the bedroom window, and she saw only white. A snow squall blocked her view of the trees behind her house. She went to the kitchen and checked the telephone, but it was dead. *I'm stranded.*

Her first thought was she had to keep warm and make a fire with the wood she'd stacked inside before the lunch gathering. Each piece seemed twice as heavy as usual. Her strength diminished; she lit the kindling and sat on the hearth, waiting for the warmth.

She realized many people might have hired Miranda to come after her, but her gut told her it was Naomi. Her body warmed as the fire roared, and her mind became more lucid. Her thoughts filled with the sounds of the bear grunting and chomping at Miranda before the woman's high-pitched squeal. It brought her no joy knowing the sick and hateful person suffered so. *There is too much hatred in the world as it is; hating her will just bring me down to her level.*

As the heat filled the room, Maddy walked to the window, wrapped in a blanket. The trail of blood was gone, buried beneath fresh snow. She wondered what the bear had done with the body.

Her stomach growled. *I need nutrition.* She went to the refrigerator, opened the door, and almost vomited, thinking of the poison that came from the creamer. Not wanting to take a chance on other tainted items, she looked in the pantry and took down peanut butter and bread. She made a sandwich and thought, *Good enough.*

She looked at the blizzard raging behind her house as she ate. Her body was regenerating; the warmth and the food were what she needed.

After eating, she went to the fireplace and fed the flames several more pieces of wood. Overwhelmed with weariness, she looked for a place to rest. She went to the recliner chair, covered herself, and shifted her body several times before falling asleep.

It was dark when she woke up. Only a few embers glowed in the fireplace, and the wood was gone. She was cold. *Shit!* Frustrated and thinking how difficult it would be to go to the basement, walk outside, and carry up more firewood, she shook her head and yearned for sleep. *I can't do this anymore.* Maddy turned over onto her side for the final nap and asked God to let her die. All she had to do was fall asleep, the cold would do the rest, and her woes would be over.

Come on, Maddy, you can do this, a voice inside her head said. *You must do this!* It was her father's voice. *Think of your daughter and Adam; they love you. Don't quit now. You're not alone; I'm here.*

"I know you are, Dad." She turned, sat up, and pushed herself out of the chair to her feet. She moaned as she forced her stiff body forward. It was dark; she felt her way to the kitchen and grabbed a flashlight from a drawer. She put on her heaviest coat and gloves and went to the basement door.

When she opened the door, she aimed the light down the stairs and was repulsed at the sight of Miranda's frozen blood. "Oh my God." Garbage and blood congealed together on the basement floor. She felt her already sick stomach waver and tried to keep the peanut butter sandwich from coming up.

Careful not to slip on the frozen blood, she held on to the handrail as she descended the stairs. When she reached the bottom, she shined the light around, grabbed a burlap wood carrier, and stepped out into the blowing snow. Snow flakes pelted her face, and her eyes blurred in the driving wind.

When she reached the woodpile, she brushed off the snow and placed eight pieces into the bag. It was too heavy to pick up, so she walked backward, dragging it through the snow to the open basement doors. Before she stepped inside, a deep, elongated guttural growl emanated inside the basement. *Oh my God, it's the bear!*

She quickly turned and dragged the wood toward the deck stairs on the other side of the house, worried the bear would come for her. *But why would he? He's eaten well and claimed my basement as his home.* She thought about how the bear had saved her life and felt affection for the beast.

Hoping she hadn't locked the back door when she reached the stairs, she lifted the heavy wood carrier one step at a time. With each tug, the bag grew heavier, and her back strained. It was dark, the wind blew hard, and her face numbed. She reached the top, turned the knob, and opened the door. *Oh, thank God,* she thought as she dragged the wood inside.

She dropped the bag on the kitchen floor, took out each piece, and brushed the snow into the sink to keep the wood from dampening, making it impossible to ignite. Each effort depleted more energy. When she finished, she started a fire and lay back in the recliner, huffing. She covered up and tried to revive herself.

Her mind drifted. Her thoughts focused on survival, and she lined up each step needed to ensure she'd make it through the ordeal. *I have to get my body temperature back up. Then I need more nutrition. If the bear tries to get inside the house, I'll need access to the Glock.* As her mind went from one issue to the next, it became heavy, and she drifted off to sleep.

A sudden, loud humming sound awakened her. She opened her eyes and heard the refrigerator motor running; the furnace was cranking the heat. *Thank God the electricity is back on.* She stayed put for a long time until she felt warm, then got up and went to the phone. The line was still dead. She realized the town would come to life, and if other awful actors looking for the ledger were in Berry Lake, they'd try to find their way to her place.

Maddy went outside, cleaned off two feet of snow from the Jeep, and started its engine to melt the rest. She left her weapon in the vehicle and the ledger in the basement. *The bear is a better guardian of the document than I am. God help anyone who tries looking for it down there while he's around.*

She knew the snow was too deep to reach Route 3 in her Jeep. Not knowing how long she'd be stranded, she did an inventory of food she felt safe eating. Once everything was in order, she went to her bed and tried giving her body the rest it needed to heal from Miranda's assault. She slept, and near noon the sound of a gas engine awoke her.

She went to the back window. A tractor with an attached snow thrower blew snow high into the air, off to the side of the road. Three pickup trucks lined up behind the tractor as the odd-looking contraption reached the house. Stick Larson jumped off, and as she walked out and approached the caravan, he yelled, "Are you okay, Maddy?" Five men and a woman got out of the trucks; Lester and Rose were among them.

Rose ran to her. "Oh, honey, you don't look well." Maddy fell into her friend's arms. She told her she didn't know how good it was to see her. The men circled, and she said Miranda Southworth had poisoned her.

"She's dead. The black bear killed her. Miranda would have killed me if it hadn't been for him."

"We were worried he might harass you because we haven't seen him elsewhere in the area," Lester said. She told them he'd made a home in her basement and might still be there.

Andy, the game warden, held a shotgun. "We need to put the animal down, Maddy." Although she knew it was necessary, she felt terrible. The poor beast had done nothing to her but kill a person who had tried to kill her.

"I can't be here for that."

"Why don't you and I go into town while they take care of the bear," Rose said. Maddy nodded, looked at everyone who came to rescue her, and realized how much the townspeople cared. She and Rose drove off. She felt a pang of sadness thinking of the bear as she saw the men moving to the side of the house.

CHAPTER 26

Naomi

Naomi paced around the old Adirondack home, frustrated and cursing at the weather. She'd tried moving her four-wheel-drive vehicle out of the driveway, but it bogged down in the snow. Having been stranded for two days, she heard an engine and ran outside, stopped a truck equipped with a snowplow, and gave a guy twenty dollars to dig out her vehicle. After shoveling the snow away from the tires and pulling with his truck, it rolled out of the rut.

Cold, she returned inside, brushed the snow off her coat, and walked to the living room by the fire. Congressman Suarez was on CNN again, talking with reporters. "Sex trafficking in America is a serious problem and must stop." Someone asked about his investigation's progress. "It will bring the people who had taken part and those responsible for trafficking innocents into the light of day." The more the man talked, the more anxious Naomi became.

The cellular phone rang. Hopeful it was Miranda, she heard, "Where's the ledger?" when she picked it up. It was the man with the gravelly voice. Naomi didn't respond, wondering how he got the phone number.

"Are you wondering how we got this number?" he laughed. "We not only have the number, we also know where you are." Then he added, "If you are not at the top of The Glades mountain at three o'clock this afternoon with the ledger, it's goodbye, Naomi." The silence seemed deafening when he hung up.

She seldom experienced panic; she always had someone else to blame or take the fall in any jam. But this time, she felt her luck running out. The tension built up in her head, and she sweated, even though it was getting cold in the house. She had to think fast. She realized she could no longer rely on The Chameleon and thought she was probably dead. Her best guess was that Reynolds had the ledger, and though she dreaded going to the despicable town of Berry Lake, she had no choice.

Fearful the people in the village might recognize her, she tried to disguise her appearance. She wore an oversized coat with a high collar, put on sunglasses, and tied her hair in a bun.

She was afraid to drive to Reynolds's house, thinking it was too dangerous. Miranda had mentioned that Reynolds was a regular at Lena's, so she parked near the place and hoped she'd find her walking in. *I'll follow her and surprise her at gunpoint wherever she stops. Then I'll force her to bring me to the ledger.* She knew her plan had holes, but she was desperate and went with it.

Berry Lake was a slimy little town in her mind, and when she arrived, it hadn't changed. Memories of the troubles it created for her and Avery flowed into her head as she crept down Main Street, looking for a strategic place to park. She found a hidden spot where she could view the diner and pulled over.

As the car ran, she watched dumpy-looking townspeople walk the streets, scoffing at how they compared to the sophisticates who populated her upscale Manhattan neighborhood. After waiting for an eternity, she grew restless, became irritable, and was ready to give up when she saw Reynolds and Rose step out of a Jeep and walk into the diner. *Now we're talking.*

CHAPTER 27

Maddy

The thought of killing the bear weighed on Maddy's mind as she and Rose drove to town. "It may sound strange, but I liked that bear. I mean, I understand him. He's a rogue, beaten up over the years and maybe sick, but he's just doing what comes naturally, trying to survive." Rose gave her a sympathetic look as though she realized her sentiment reflected Maddy's own life.

They pulled up to Lena's, went inside, and the place was empty. They sat in a booth near a front window, and Rose said she must be worried about Adam. "It seems like he's been on assignment forever. I fear he's into something serious."

"Say some prayers. That's what I do when I'm afraid." Maddy didn't say it, but she'd been doing a lot of it. She began feeling better and asked for a pitcher of ice water. She drank the entire amount, letting it cleanse her body.

"How about you? You're always concerned for everyone else. How are things going with you and Jed?" Rose looked to the side as though she was embarrassed, then said her husband had lost his job at the mill.

"I think we're headed for hard times. It's the damn alcohol. He just can't stay away. I love the guy, but God knows he doesn't make it easy."

It was the first time Maddy had heard her friend express sadness. She always seemed to put a cheerful face on things, no matter how bad. "He's lucky to have you."

"Look, it's Andy's pickup." Rose pointed outside. The game warden drove by with a blue tarp draped over something in the back.

"It looks like they killed the bear," Maddy said. "I guess I should get you home, then head back to my place. I feel like hell and have an enormous mess to clean up."

They walked out, and when they got in the Jeep, a voice in the back seat said, "I have a gun to Rose's head. Don't turn around; just drive to your house, Reynolds." It was Naomi.

Rose gazed straight ahead, looking stiffer than an icicle and her eyes glaring with fear. *Don't panic, Rose,* Maddy thought, hoping her friend, who had no experience in such matters, wouldn't cause the evil woman to pull the trigger.

Naomi sat up when they left the village. "I have little time and less patience. I want the ledger. Don't test me on this. When we get to your place, you go inside, bring it out, and I'll stay with Rose." The ledger was important to Maddy, but not as important as Rose. She drove to the top of the hill, and Naomi told them to get out. Rose stood with her hands raised like she was being robbed.

"What makes you think I have the ledger?" Naomi pointed the gun at Rose, pulled the trigger, and a loud bang rang out across the open space between the hills. Rose fell over onto her side, screaming. "Oh, Maddy!" Maddy ran to her as blood oozed out onto the shoulder of her white coat. Rose began sobbing. Maddy held her, gave her a comforting caress, then stared at Naomi.

"That's showing you I'm not fucking around. Get in that house, and if you don't return with the ledger, I'll kill you both."

"You're going to be okay, Rose. You're hit in the shoulder; no vitals there. I'll be right back." She got up with her eyes riveted on Naomi and walked into the house.

After the bear dragged Miranda away, she had one Glock remaining. It was in the door panel, but Maddy wasn't about to take any chances. She went to the basement, fished out the ledger, and brought it outside.

"See all that gets done when you apply a little pressure," Naomi said with a snarky sneer as she took the book.

Rose was bleeding, and her face looked a sickly shade of white. Maddy said she needed to dress her wound. "She'll be fine; get in your car. We're going up to The Glades mountain. We have to meet someone in fifteen minutes. Move it." Maddy helped Rose into the Jeep. The woman shivered as she tried to calm her. "You'll be alright, I promise."

Naomi got into the back seat. As Maddy drove, her mind went to the Glock in the door panel next to her. There was no room for error, and she nixed the idea of trying to take out Naomi while in the car.

Rose slumped to her side, whimpering as she leaned on the car door. The Jeep drove through the village, and when they reached the road up the mountain, Naomi said, "When we get to the top, Rose can stay in the car; you do what I tell you, and no games."

The town had cleared the road of snow, and when they reached the top, a black Chevy Suburban sat with its engine running. Four men got out of the enormous vehicle.

"Okay, Reynolds, out of the car."

"What about Rose? She needs medical attention."

Naomi pointed the gun at her face and shouted, "Out of the fucking car, I said."

As Maddy opened the Jeep door, she glanced at the Glock in the panel and thought how easy it would be to kill the wretched woman. The men standing nearby, however, had guns. *Not a good idea, Maddy.*

She walked around her vehicle with Naomi a half step behind, holding the ledger and pointing the weapon. When Maddy looked at the four men, her stomach did a backflip; Adam was among them. Long-haired and bearded, he wore a ski cap and a down coat. He held a pistol in his right hand. Maddy's body wanted to scream with joy, and for an instant, their eyes locked, but her fear overtook her sensibilities, and she looked away.

Her next thought was that Naomi might recognize Adam from when he was undercover at The Glades.

"That's far enough," a man with a face like steel said. He had no expression; his cold black eyes seemed to project power and lacked human feeling. *He's the boss*, Maddy realized.

"Louie, get the ledger." A tall man with broad shoulders and a bald head walked to Naomi, and she handed over the book.

"Should I take her weapon, Nemo?" The boss nodded.

"Pauly, check it out."

The shortest thug took the book, opened it, and inspected the pages. "This is it, boss."

"Sam, take the woman and bring her into the car," Nemo ordered. Maddy piped up and said a wounded woman in the Jeep needed attention. "Bring that woman too, Sam."

Sam, who was Adam, walked past Naomi. She gawked at him and said, "I know you; you're Bob. You worked for Avery at The Glades."

Maddy noticed the bald man, Louie, squinting. "I don't know no fucking Avery," Adam snapped, taking Maddy's arm and shoving her toward the Jeep. "Get the wounded woman," he barked to her.

When Maddy opened the rear door, Rose lay with her eyes open. She was in a daze as she shivered, unaware of her surroundings. Maddy shook her. "Come on, Rose, we have to move. I'll help you." She struggled to get the woman out of the vehicle, drooped one of Rose's arms over her shoulder, and hobbled with her toward the Suburban. Adam, remaining perfect in his role as Sam, walked close behind with his gun pointing at her. Maddy noticed Naomi gazing at Adam as they passed by, trying to determine if he was the Bob who worked for Avery Jordan.

When they got to the Suburban, Adam opened the back door and helped Maddy get Rose into the third row. He whispered, "I hope we can pull this off. I think Louie's suspicious." He moved to the next row of seats toward the front, holding his gun on Maddy, and said they were going to kill Naomi.

Maddy looked through the back window. The three men faced the albino as she became animated, shaking her hands and yelling before turning and running. Two men fired their weapons in tandem. The top of the woman's head separated from her body and flew into the air. Her skull cap, with its white-hair bun, landed ten feet away. Naomi lay in a bloody mess.

"That was the plan. But they weren't expecting you and Rose, and I don't know what they'll do. Be prepared for anything."

When the men returned to the car, Pauly got behind the wheel. As Maddy tried comforting Rose in the back, Nemo, the boss, sat in the passenger seat, and Louie, the big man with a bald head, sat next to Adam in the middle row.

Nemo turned, looked back at Maddy, and asked, "How bad is she?"

"The bleeding stopped, but an infection will set in without an antibiotic."

"We're headed to Utica. She'll have to wait until then." Then he added, "You're Reynolds, right?" She said she was. "You did good taking out that creep, Cupid." With that, the mob boss turned and looked out the front window.

Louie kept turning and looking back at Maddy as they drove. "So you're the big shot detective who doesn't like child-killers. Guess what? I killed a kid once. It wasn't much fun; she cried like a baby and died too quick." He smiled, and Maddy's stomach roiled, remembering how Cupid tortured children before killing them. She turned her head and tried ignoring the neanderthal man.

She glimpsed Adam looking straight ahead, and he seemed unmoved by the guy's comment. *Good Adam.*

Tension ran through her veins, worried about Rose and wondering if the men in the car suspected Adam wasn't who he was pretending to be. She also wondered if they were using their real names because if they were, they would not let her go and would kill her. They knew Rose was unconscious and was no threat, but Maddy was vulnerable.

CHAPTER 28

Hannah

When the helicopter landed in Tupper Lake, the snow had stopped falling, the sun shone, and it was cold. Ethan led Hannah to an old schoolhouse, abandoned three years earlier, for the modern facility outside of town.

"We're setting up the gym. It's adequate for what we need." He was referring to its accommodations as a command-and-control center. He opened the door, and she could still see her breath when she walked into the ample space. "We're working on the heat," he said.

Hannah walked to a table where five operational support technicians, each with phones to their ears, gathered and compiled information. The supervisor monitoring activity at the table explained, "We should have a situation assessment within minutes." Hannah nodded, moved to a folding table to be used as a makeshift desk, sat, and looked over the previous status reports.

The only new information was from a game warden who reported to the New York State Department of Environmental Conservation that a bear had to be put down in Berry Lake. Something caught her eye as she was about to cast aside the irrelevant information. *Euthanasia occurred at the residence of Madison Reynolds under extenuating circumstances, still needing to be determined.*

"Ethan, did you see this?"

"Yes, we're trying to figure out the extenuating circumstances."

A knot began forming in the center of Hannah's stomach, as it always did whenever she heard language like 'extenuating circumstances still needing to be determined.'

"Where are we with the mobile units?"

Looking at his watch, Ethan said they should be arriving in Berry Lake now. A woman working the phones raised her hand. He went to her, looked over her shoulder, read what she'd written, and brought the paper to Hannah. "They found Naomi White's body at The Glades Memorial; she was shot several times in the head. Maddy Reynolds's Jeep was nearby, and blood covered the passenger seat."

The knot in Hannah's stomach now tugged at her abdomen. "Do we have any idea where she is?"

"No, we don't."

"She couldn't just disappear into thin air, for Christ's sake," Hannah shouted, distraught over losing the only person she needed to track.

Sara, an agent working with Ethan on the case, shouted, "We have a report of a black Chevy Suburban that drove through town late in the afternoon. No one recognized the vehicle; no one has seen it since."

"Then Reynolds is not in Berry Lake," Hannah thundered, so everyone in the room could hear. "They killed Naomi White, mob style. Whoever took her out was in the Suburban and has Reynolds." She ordered Sara to compile a list of black Chevy Suburban owners in the Utica area. "These guys must be out of Utica."

An operation technician, who waited for her to finish, handed Ethan a sheet of paper. He read it as Hannah stood waiting for the update. "The state troopers have lost track of Adam Forsyth; the last they knew, he was in Berry Lake. That was three hours ago."

Hannah twisted her lips, then said, "Reynolds and Forsyth are in that Chevy. They have to be headed to Utica. Contact the Oneida County Sheriff's Office, and get me Captain Zepatello."

"One of our agents in the village of Berry Lake is on the phone, and he says it's urgent," a woman working a phone shouted. Hannah and Ethan went to the table and stood around the technician. She told her to put the agent on speaker.

"This is Hannah Bates; who am I speaking with?"

"This is Senior Agent Banks."

"What do you have, Banks?"

"We've interviewed several local men who said they'd been to Maddy Reynolds's home earlier today to put down a rogue black bear that had found its way into the basement."

"What's so urgent about that?"

"The bear killed a woman and dragged the body into the woods. They said they knew the woman as Miranda Southworth, and Maddy Reynolds told them Southworth poisoned her."

"They spoke to Maddy Reynolds?"

"Yes, she and a woman named Rose Gilly drove off together in Reynolds's Jeep. They were at Lena's diner in the village for a while. It was the last anyone has seen of them."

"Good work, Banks. Let us know when you get a positive ID on Miranda Southworth." Hannah knew Southworth had to be Hilda Heinrich. The Goddess of Death, as her boss referred to Hilda, also known as The Chameleon, was an expert with various drugs.

How did Reynolds get a bear to kill The Chameleon after being poisoned?

People came at Hannah, one after another, with updates. The flurry of activity was like electricity in the air; the abandoned school gymnasium was alive. "Special Agent Bates, we have Captain Zepatello on the line," Sara shouted to her, handing a phone over.

"Frank, it's Hannah Bates."

"Hey, Hannah, what ya got?"

"We've got a black Chevy Suburban out of Berry Lake that we think is headed to Utica. The passengers include an unknown number of mob guys, one undercover trooper detective named Adam Forsyth, and two women, one of whom has likely sustained a gunshot wound. The women are Rose Gilly and Maddy Reynolds."

"Come again, on the last name?"

"Yes, it's Maddy, Zep."

"Oh, Jesus." After a long silence, he said, "We'll be looking for the Suburban and will notify the hospitals to be on the lookout for a gunshot wound and report it to us."

"We're already compiling a list of Suburban owners in the area. We'll get it over when we have it." Although Hannah knew Maddy had become Zep's protégé detective during the Cupid investigation, and she was dear to his heart, there was nothing more to be said under the circumstances. They hung up.

She looked around the room. The FBI team, who assembled on short notice, worked well together, and she was pleased. The activity plateaued in the evening, and she stepped outdoors to get some air. It was dark, and the outside smelled good compared to the musty old building. Though freezing, the still mountain air revived her. She walked in the dark, contemplating the case's complexity, and thought back to when Maddy first asked for her help with The Glades.

Hannah had balked, not wanting to get involved, afraid of the political ramifications that might result. Bigwigs had touted The Glades as a playground for the very rich and esteemed. That was before the dark underside of its sex trafficking came to light.

She walked toward the frozen lake, stopped, and looked over the vast space. *The ledger has shaken the hornets from their nests, and they've converged on Maddy Reynolds.*

CHAPTER 29

Maddy

Rose lay with her head on Maddy's lap as the Suburban cruised toward Utica. She was burning up with a fever, and Maddy knew she'd be in trouble if she didn't get her to a hospital soon. "Nemo," she called out. The boss man in the front turned and looked into the back. "Rose is very sick; if we don't get her to a hospital, we might lose her." Nemo mumbled a few words to Pauly, who was driving, and said nothing more.

She tried to comfort Rose as best she could, stroking her hair and wiping sweat from her face with a tissue. She noticed the tension in Adam, who was sitting erect and tapping his fingers with his outstretched hands on the back of the seat. She wondered if Naomi's comment about his working for Avery Jordan may have rattled him, and she spoke to him in her head. *Don't do anything, Adam, or you'll blow our cover.*

The car phone rang, and Pauly answered. "Hello. He's right here." He handed it to Nemo. "It's the big guy."

"Yes, we have it," Nemo said. "Pauly checked it out, and it's the real thing." There was silence while he listened to instructions, then he said okay and hung up. Maddy noticed they were entering the city of Utica and wondered where they were going. Adam's tapping fingers made her anxious, and she worried he might try to intervene, but she knew that with three armed bad guys and only Adam with a gun, it would end in disaster.

Her attention turned to her friend. Rose lay with her eyes closed, wheezing. Filled with guilt, she whispered, "I'm so sorry, dear friend. You didn't realize that being my friend would bring such heartache, did you?" She closed her eyes and became lost in the silence of her mind for a moment. The car slowed; Maddy opened her eyes and saw a sign that read, *St. Elizabeth's Hospital, Emergency Entrance.*

Pauly stopped the car, got out, went inside, and minutes later, two men dressed in blue scrubs came out with a wheelchair. He opened the door. "These men will take Rose." Maddy got out of the car as the orderlies lifted Rose and placed her in the wheelchair.

"Get back in," Pauly yelped. He bolted to the driver's door, jumped inside, and took off. She looked out the rear window to see Rose slumped over in the wheelchair and the two men in scrubs with their mouths open, looking at Pauly speeding away. *That's one way to get things done*, she thought.

It was dark as they drove through the city. Louie kept turning his head, looking at her and smiling. She knew the bald man had an agenda of his own and hoped the boss would keep him under control.

When they arrived at an abandoned industrial park, empty railroad cars covered with rust and graffiti stood in the dark like artifacts from a bygone era. The Suburban sped by empty warehouses, slowed, and pulled into an open garage door. Two men wearing ski hats waited, and the garage door closed when the Suburban pulled inside. Nemo and Pauly stayed in the front seat. Louie pulled his weapon, pointed it at Adam, and told Maddy to get out. He took Adam's gun and said, "You too, Sam."

Her heart dropped; Adam's cover was blown. One of the two men with ski hats came to Maddy, and the other went with Louie. The garage door opened, and the Suburban backed out as Pauly and Nemo remained inside the car. As the guy led Maddy to a room at gunpoint, her and Adam's eyes met. Her heart twisted into a knot; the pain almost brought her to her knees. She knew it was the last time they would see one another alive.

The room was poorly lit, windowless, and about ten by ten. It had faded yellow paint and a single bench across the back wall. A steel door slammed shut, and the sound of a deadbolt clunked closed when she walked in. She stood alone in numb disbelief, her arms hanging limp, helpless to stop what she knew was about to happen; she fell to her knees.

Voices echoed in the open space of the warehouse as men argued. They grew louder. There was shuffling, and Maddy knew Adam was fighting for his life. Pounding on the door, she screamed his name, wanting to be with him. A loud bang was followed by complete silence, and she knew Adam was dead. She went numb. All hope and reason for living vanished. Wishing to die with her lover, she screamed a long, drawn-out "No!"

She wailed from her depths. An endless river of pain ran through her body until nothing remained. She sat on the floor, leaning against the bench with no feeling, only a chasm where once there was Adam.

The garage door opened, and she listened to the sound of a car driving in, stopping, and in a few minutes, driving out again. *Adam's in the trunk*, she thought. The garage door closed, and the only words Maddy's soul could eke out were, "Farewell, my love."

CHAPTER 30

Hannah

It was early evening, and Hannah hadn't slept the night before. The wooden cots had been uncomfortable and hurt her back; she was on edge. She poured coffee into a styrofoam cup, blew off the steam to cool it, and walked to a window. *This place is colder than cold.* She watched the sunlight disappear into a haze lying over frozen Tupper Lake.

At about eight at night, a call came in from one of Zepatello's detectives, Al Ramirez. He said Rose Gilly from Berry Lake had been admitted to St. Elizabeth's Hospital with a gunshot wound. She was undergoing surgery, and they'd be interviewing her. Ramirez said they'd be back in touch when they finished.

"Where's Ethan?" Hannah called out. Sara said he was catching some sleep. "Wake him, please." Ethan came out, running his fingers through his hair as though only half awake. She asked how long it would take to drive to Utica, and he said a little over two hours. "Let's go; you drive. Sara, contact the sheriffs down there and ask them to hold off on Gilly's interview until we arrive. Send any updates to my cell phone."

She and Ethan scurried to one of the unmarked mobile units and headed south. Her mind raced. *Who are these guys? One of the Utica mafia families? We got to get a make on that damn Suburban. Where the hell are they keeping Reynolds?* Her only comforting thought was that Adam was with Maddy and might give her an edge in a confrontation.

The phone rang. Zepatello was on the line, and Hannah put it on speaker. "How far are you from St. Elizabeth's?" She looked at Ethan, and he mouthed *twenty minutes*.

"We're twenty minutes away."

"Gilly got out of surgery a few hours ago. We can talk to her anytime. She's quite shaken up but will talk to us. We'll be waiting in the lobby when you arrive."

Ethan let Hannah off in front of the hospital, and she went inside while he parked the car. Zep and Al Ramirez stood in the lobby, looking concerned.

Hannah understood that Maddy Reynolds was more than a retiree to the detectives; she had become their lifelong friend. The city of Utica celebrated when Maddy killed Cupid, a man who had been raping and murdering its children. Not only would the police department grieve if anything terrible happened to her, but the entire community would be heartbroken.

"It looks like Maddy's in deep shit," Zep said when she walked over. "At least she has Forsyth with her. Do you know if she's injured?"

"We believe she's been poisoned. We don't know the shape she's in." Zep and Al looked at each other with fear and anger. Zep turned to the woman at the front desk, showed her his badge, and said they were there to see Rose Gilly. When Ethan joined them, the four took the elevator to the fifth floor.

Rose lay with her shoulder bandaged and eyes closed when they walked in. The woman seemed still affected by sedation, and Zep suggested maybe it would be best if only he and Hannah conducted the interview. When they approached the bedside, Rose opened her eyes.

"We're from law enforcement. This is Hannah Bates with the FBI, and I'm Frank Zepatello with the Oneida County Sheriffs." Rose looked at Zep, tried to smile, and said Maddy had talked much about him over the years. She asked if Maddy was alright.

"She is still with the men who brought you to Utica," Hannah said. "We are trying to find her."

Rose's eyebrows curled, and she turned to the window. "Oh, dear."

"Why don't you tell us what happened when you and Maddy were with Naomi White."

She took deep breaths, wiggled around in the bed to get comfortable, and began. "Naomi was hiding in Maddy's Jeep when we left Lena's. She held a gun to my head and made Maddy drive to her place. When we got there, she shot me just to show us she wasn't fucking around; excuse my language. She wanted the ledger. Maddy went inside, brought it out, and gave it to her. I don't remember much after that."

Hannah asked what had happened to the ledger. "I think the men took it."

"Explain about the men."

"We went to The Glades Memorial, where there were men. I don't know how many, but I think they took it. I'm sorry, I just can't remember much after that."

"Think hard," Zep said. "There must be something else you can recall." She looked out the window and was silent for a long while. "Nemo. I remember Maddy calling out to a guy in the car named Nemo." Hannah and Zep locked eyes; *Holy shit, can it be?* Hannah thought.

"Are you sure the name you heard was Nemo, not Nino?"

"I'm pretty sure it was Nemo." Rose, pale and weakened, leaned her head to the side and stared into space as though spent. Hannah thanked her and said she'd done a lot to help her friend.

Zep and Hannah stepped into the hall, where Ethan and Al waited. "Nemo Zerilli is Mario Lutanza's right-hand man," Hannah said. "Lutanza is out of New Orleans and runs the entire East Coast underworld." She turned to Ethan and asked him to contact the command center. "Have them talk to the people who saw the Suburban. Find out if they noticed the color of the plates."

As she and Ethan drove back with Al and Zep, Hannah realized she had misjudged who she was pursuing. When they arrived at the Sheriff's Department, she called field agents to find Mario Lutanza's connection with the ledger. She learned he'd lost millions on The Glades when Avery Jordan killed himself and failed to pay off his note. The lost money was not his biggest concern. Instead, he worried about politicians who ran interference for him named in the ledger. If exposed, he and they would end up in prison.

She slumped back into her desk chair, exhausted, and looked at her watch. It was too late to say goodnight to her son, but she thought her husband might be awake and called home. "Hello, Sigmund." Anthony answered and said he was just about to turn off the lights.

"Catch any bad guys?"

"Not yet, but we're working on it." They said they loved each other, and when they hung up, Hannah felt an old familiar pain that tugged at her insides whenever she was away from her family.

Zep popped his head in the office doorway and said they were about to interview an informant in the interrogation room. Hannah got up and followed. As they walked down a hallway, Zep explained the guy was Tommy Tutts and hung down at Bucky's Cigar Shop. "There's illegal betting going on down there, but we turn a blind eye for occasions like this. We know where we can find them when we need them."

They grabbed Ethan on the way, and he followed them into the observation room. On the other side of the mirror, Al sat at a table across from a skinny guy with a scruffy goatee and long, stringy hair.

"What we have here is at least a misdemeanor." Al held a plastic bag with what appeared to be a small amount of weed.

"Aww, come on, Detective Ramirez. There's not enough there to get high on. Why don't you just tell me what you're looking for instead of busting my balls?"

Al placed the bag on the table. "We are looking for guys new to the area within the last few days. They're from New Orleans." Tutts looked down at the floor, appearing scared.

"I don't know nobody like that."

"Tommy, you're on parole. A misdemeanor right now will put you back behind bars. You don't want that, do you?"

The guy curled his lips, his eyebrows furled, and he seemed to concentrate on assessing the risks inherent in his decision. He took a deep breath and exhaled. "Okay, but you guys can get me killed if they find out I talked to you. These are some bad motherfuckers." Hannah and Zep glanced at each other as though realizing the seriousness of Maddy's situation.

"There's this guy. His name is Pauly. He's been placing bets down at the cigar store all day today. I heard him say when his trifecta came in, he was blowing New Orleans and headed for the Bahamas, where the girls are hot and easy."

Zep barged into the room. "Grab Tutts, and let's get down to Bucky's." They rushed to the parking lot. Zep, Hannah, and Ethan went in Zep's unmarked car, and Al drove with Tutts in the back seat. When they arrived, they parked down the street from the cigar store.

Al's voice came over Zep's radio. "Tutts thinks the guy will return to pick up his winnings before the cigar store closes at midnight."

"Okay, let's sit tight and wait," Zep said. He turned to Hannah. "I can't believe this is happening to Maddy again. She's had more than her fair share of bad guys trying to kill her. I don't know what this town will do if she doesn't make it." Hannah looked at him, knowing his affection for the remarkable woman.

Her cell phone rang, and she answered. "This is Special Agent Bates. We have identified Miranda Southworth. Her real name was Hilda Heinrich, a.k.a. The Goddess of Death or The Chameleon."

"That's what I thought. Thanks, Bates." She shared the information with Zep and said the woman came after Maddy because of the ledger. He asked if she had any idea how someone like Heinrich might have gotten recruited. She told him Naomi White hired her. "They found White dead in Berry Lake."

Al's voice came over the radio again. "That's the guy, the one with a ponytail."

"Okay. Let Tommy go. You and I will get the guy."

After letting Tutts out of the back seat, Al and Zep entered the cigar store while Hannah and Ethan waited in the car. She watched as the two men came out, each holding one of the guy's arms. He tried to wiggle out of their grip, but Zep and Al slammed him against the building. Hannah winced, concerned about police brutality. The guy soon submitted, and they put him in the back seat of Al's car. Both cars started back to headquarters.

She realized the Utica detectives were casting aside rules, regulations, and the law to save their friend, but she kept her druthers to herself. After they secured the guy when they arrived at headquarters, they were about to interview him when Zep got a call. He hung up and said he had to handle something. "I'll be back in ten."

Hannah and Ethan waited, but the minutes turned into an hour. When Zep returned, and they were heading to the interrogation room to interview the guy with the ponytail, a detective handed Zep a slip of paper.

"Shit!" He turned to Hannah. "We'll have to wait. I have to identify a body." Hannah asked if she and Ethan could tag along. "Of course."

He drove with Al in the front seat and Hannah and Ethan in the back. Hannah began recalibrating her theory of which mob guys she was pursuing. *It makes sense Mario Lutanza's operation is running the show.* She remembered Avery Jordan and Naomi White started out in New Orleans. *Lutanza bankrolled The Glades for Jordan, I bet. His political connections in the ledger are freaking out about now, fearing exposure.*

Zep pulled into a park. The moon was bright, and a few people stood around with cross-country skis leaning against them at the far end of a parking lot. A half dozen police cars with lights flashing cordoned off an area. Bud Renshaw, one of Zep's senior detectives and a devoted friend of Maddy Reynolds, walked up as Zep, Hannah, and Ethan got out.

Zep introduced him to the FBI agents, and Bud told Hannah he remembered her. "You came to Maddy's retirement party to tell her the Donnollys escaped from Dannemora and were coming to kill her." Hannah remembered. It was another horrific event in Maddy's life.

"What ya got, Bud?" Zep asked.

"Those women were cross-country skiing and ran across a body in the woods." He pointed to a clump of trees. "The body's fresh; it's still warm." He handed Zep a polaroid picture as Hannah looked on. A skinny man with a scruffy goatee and long, stringy hair lay in the snow. He had a hole in the side of his head where blood oozed out. "It's Tommy Tutts," Bud said.

"Holy shit. Someone must have seen him get out of the car at Bucky's. These guys aren't fucking around." Zep looked at Hannah. "If the men who have Maddy are from New Orleans, that's where they'll take her to kill her. The mob in this town would never want Maddy Reynolds found assassinated here. There'd be an outcry, and sympathetic people would turn on them."

"Are we talking about Maddy Reynolds here?" Bud asked, surprised, looking at Al as if it were the first he'd heard his friend was in the crosshairs of death. Al nodded, and Bud clenched his fists.

Bud had scoffed at Maddy, the first female detective in the department. He had hated the notion of women detectives. He thought they'd need to be pampered and might get a guy killed when the shit came down. That attitude ended the night Maddy dived into a room, killing Benny Bowles when the guy had the drop on her. Bud was with her and was man enough to admit he was wrong; he had stood by Maddy ever since. Everyone had heard the story, including Hannah, who marveled at the loyalty Maddy had garnered among her ex-compadres.

"Have you checked the tire tracks?" Zep asked.

Bud hesitated, looking as if he was still in disbelief at what Al had just told him. He pulled a ziplock bag from his pocket and handed it over. "We found this in the tire tracks. They had to be made by the perpetrator's vehicle because there are no other tracks in this area."

Al held a flashlight as Zep inspected the material in the bag. He moved tiny black granules and a white, ash-like substance mixed with soil in his hand. "This is coal and potash. There are dozens of abandoned industrial sites around Utica, but only a few transported coal and potash. Wherever this came from is where Maddy is."

"How likely is it they intend to kill Maddy?" Al asked Hannah.

"Almost definitely," Hannah said. "They wouldn't have used their real names in front of her if they planned on letting her go. The probability of finding her alive if they get her to New Orleans is diminished. We have to stop them."

"We need to get back and interview the ponytail guy," Zep said. "Al, when we get back, identify every industrial park in the area that transported coal and potash."

When they returned to headquarters, they placed the guy with the ponytail in the interrogation room with his hands cuffed behind his back. This time, Zep conducted the interview as Bud stood by. Hannah and Ethan watched from the observation room. She noticed Bud seemed agitated as the enormous man stood nearby with his fists clenched and face tightened.

Zep asked the guy for his name. "None of your fucking business," he replied while smiling.

"It's Paul Zimmerman." Bud was looking at papers from his wallet.

"Hey, you can't do that. I want a lawyer."

"You'll get your lawyer, but first, we have a few questions." The interview was illegal, but under the circumstances, with time running out on Maddy Reynolds's life, Hannah kept silent.

Zep cut to the chase. "We know you were in a car with Maddy Reynolds, and we want to know where she is." The guy laughed and said nothing. Hannah noticed Bud's face growing as red as his hair. "We'll make your life goddamn miserable unless you tell us where she is." Hannah cringed, noticing Ethan's uneasy glare as he watched Zep's unconventional methods.

Pauly sat up as though he were about to leap out of his seat. "You don't know who you're fucking around with!"

Bud exploded. The tall man reached out, grabbed Pauly by his hair, lifted him out of his chair, and screamed, "You little fuck, you're the one who doesn't know who he's fucking around with!"

Hannah saw Al jump into the room to help Zep pull the guy out of Bud's grip. "Get him out of here," Zep said to Al; he and Bud left the room. Pauly's face was red, his eyes bulged, and he sweated. Ethan looked at Hannah, and she put her hands up as though telling him to just wait and let them do their job.

Al returned to the room, and Zep continued. "What you don't understand, Pauly, is Maddy Reynolds took out a serial killer in this town.

If we were to put the word out on the street that you guys have her and intend on harming her, you'll be dead before you get to the New York State Thruway; get it?"

Pauly asked if he could have a cigarette as he trembled. Zep told Al to take the cuffs off. Al released the guy's hands and pulled out a pack of smokes. Pauly took one, and Al lit it for him. He took a deep drag and exhaled. Zep let him calm down and started up again. "So, why don't you tell us what you know? We don't care about any other shit you guys have been involved with; all we want is Reynolds."

Pauly took another drag, leaned on the table with his forearms, and started talking. "It might be too late. She might already be dead." Hannah saw Zep's change of expression. His eyes squinted, his jowls bulged, and the veins on his forehead stuck out. Yet he remained quiet and let the guy talk.

"Nemo, the guy I work for, told Louie to take care of Reynolds. Louie's going to kill her here in Utica tonight, and we'll take the body in the trunk of a car to New Orleans. Louie said if we drive right through all night, it shouldn't stink too bad by the time we get there." Zep looked like he was about to jump across the table and strangle the guy, but he refrained. Pauly chuckled and added, "Louie's got the hots for her. He said he's going to fuck her before he kills her."

Ice ran through Hannah's veins. "We've got to find her before it's too late."

Zep held his cool and seemed to calm down before saying, "Where are they keeping Reynolds?"

"In some warehouse. I don't know where it is. I just followed directions. I couldn't find the place again if you paid me." Zep asked him to describe the area. "There were lots of railroad tracks and old rail cars; that's all I know."

"What about Nemo? Where is he?" The guy clammed up, looking like the question hit a nerve. Bud stepped back into the room and handed a slip of paper to Zep.

"I found this parking pass for the Ramada Inn in his jacket." Pauly turned his head, glaring at the pass. "Alright, Al and Bud, take this scumbag out of here and lock him up. Then you two get a few detectives and get over to the Ramada Inn. You're looking for Dominick Zerilli, a.k.a. Nemo."

"Oh, Al, where are we on that list of warehouses?"

"Sally was working on it. I asked her to put it on my desk when she finished."

Al and Bud took Pauly and left the room. Hannah and Ethan met Zep in the hallway, and before leaving the building, Zep grabbed the list from Al's desk.

Hannah didn't like Zep's tactics but trusted his ability to get things done, and at that moment, their interests aligned; they needed to find Maddy before Louie killed her.

When they got in the car, Zep said, "It looks like only two industrial parks transported coal and potash. Let's hope we're lucky and hit the jackpot with the first one."

Hannah watched as the neighborhoods became more decrepit the farther they went. It was dark outside, but the snow illuminated the area, and brown brick buildings were covered with graffiti and glassless windows lined up in rows. Al's voice came over the radio as Zep's car crept between two of the abandoned buildings.

"It looks like Nemo hired the Tucker brothers to help with the operation." Zep looked over and told Hannah the Tuckers were two local goons who sometimes worked jobs for the mob.

Al continued. "When we arrived, they were walking out of the hotel. We questioned them; they were carrying, so we searched them. Each had ten new hundred-dollar bills in their pocket. They caved when we told them what Nemo planned on doing to Maddy. They told us Zerilli had a document on a desk that said *The Glades* when they went to his room to collect their money."

Hannah whispered to Zep that, since they now had probable cause, his men needed to take the room by force. "The first thing Zerilli will do if he has time is head for the bathroom and burn the ledger." Zep conveyed the information to Al and Bud.

"We're going in now; wish us luck."

Hannah wondered why Zerilli hadn't already destroyed the ledger; it would have eliminated all threats of exposure for the men listed inside. Then she realized Lutanza intended to leverage the document to control his political connections, perhaps even reverting to blackmail.

"Thank God it snowed a little today," Zep said as he drove by the fourth building in the industrial park. "Few people travel through here, so any tire tracks we see might be where we'll find Maddy." When they scanned the seventh and last building, he said it looked like they struck out. He headed to the main drag and then to Schiller Works, the second location on Al's list.

As he sped through city streets with lights flashing, but no siren, Al's voice came over the radio again. "We got it! Nemo didn't give it up without a fight. Bud and the guy shot it out with each other. Nemo is still alive by a thread. Bud has a minor wound."

"How bad?" Zep asked.

"The bullet grazed his scalp; it was a close one. We're going to Schiller Works; we'll meet you there."

"Tell Bud he needs to get to a hospital now; I mean it," Zep said.

"Zep, neither you nor I can stop him from being where Maddy is; I tried."

"Son of a bitch," Zep said, frustrated. Hannah thought Zep was like a captain in a military unit, directing his men, yet always trying to watch out for them. She thought he carried his reputation from Vietnam with him into civilian life and had earned everyone's respect by doing so.

When they reached Schiller Works, it started snowing. "This damn snow will cover tire tracks. We have to hurry." He sped up and turned on the bright lights. He drove down the first of a dozen long buildings, circled around, and returned down the other side. On the fourth pass, still visible in the snow, tire tracks led to an open garage door. "Let's hope this is it." He pulled over.

Hannah's stomach was in knots. She got out and pulled her weapon from its holster, and the three eased their way to the warehouse door opening.

CHAPTER 31

Maddy

Lost in her private darkness, Maddy sat on the floor, resting her head on her outstretched arm, propped up by the bench along the back wall. *This is it; it all comes to this.* Even the pain from Miranda's torture was light years away from where she was now. Her mind knew what had happened to Adam, but her heart closed its eyes, refusing to see it.

Hey babe, she heard herself say as she sat in the dark the night before the conference in the Washington hotel room. Adam was so tired. They'd been up late the night before, making love and thinking they'd always have each other. *But it never works out that way,* a voice inside said. It was that way with her father, too. He'd left the house in the morning, and his last words to her were, *See you tonight, Maddy.* She never heard his voice again.

I want this to be over, Dad. I don't want to go on anymore. An inkling of sorrow found its way into her consciousness. Behind it, a torrent of pain burst out from deep inside. Again, she wept. Each bellow brought her closer to the gaping hole Adam had left. *Oh, how can this be? My poor Adam.*

Semiconscious, she fell deeper into the abyss, that dark place where all of one's pain sleeps. Her mind realized where her broken heart was taking her; it led to death. *A battle is taking place inside of you,* her mind told her. *You must decide whether you want to go on living or fall into the restful place where there is eternal peace.* Maddy wanted peace. She heard children's voices as she contemplated the road she needed to choose.

The image of two little girls straddling tricycles came into her mind. *I'm Brandi. My sister is Tara. She's shy; she don't talk to people she don't know.* Maddy recognized the girls from Bleeker Road but didn't understand the vision. She looked at the children smiling at her, and a woman appeared behind them. It was their mother, but the woman's face blurred.

It wasn't the woman from Bleeker Road. Maddy gazed in bewilderment as the faces of the children changed, and their mother became clear. *Oh, my God, it's Amber.* She knew the girls were her unborn grandchildren, and she felt her father's presence showing her what she had to live for.

With the sound of footsteps, the lock clunked, and the steel door opened. Louie, the bald man with broad shoulders, stood in the doorway, smiling. His arms hung to his sides, and he clutched a long, shiny blade in one hand.

The ordeal with Miranda had weakened Maddy, and a confrontation with the large man seemed overwhelming. "Hi," he whispered as his eyes roamed over her body. He looked like a starving man drooling over a steak dinner. "I kind of like you."

She felt the adrenaline entering her body, but it would take more than physical strength to survive an assault by the powerful man. She called upon her most potent weapon — her mind.

Louie stepped toward her, placed the blade to her throat, and licked her face. She didn't move. "I have a present for you." He pulled a photo out of his shirt pocket. Maddy and Adam stood together on a summer day. "Your boyfriend didn't die easy. He kept this in his wallet. You must have done him real good. Now you can do me good, too."

She looked at Adam's face in the photo and wanted the bald man dead. She felt the strength of indignation. Like a parent lifting a three-thousand-pound car to free their child, power exploded throughout her body. In one movement, she snapped one hand to push the knife to the side and penetrated Louie's eyes with the fingers of her other hand. He screamed. As she held the hand with the knife, she felt his testicles crunch when she drove her knee into his groin. He dropped, and she ran from the room.

She went to the vehicle, looking for the keys, but they were not in sight. She hit the garage-opener button, bolting toward the door, and it opened slowly. In the reflection of the car window, she saw Louie struggle to his feet. Unable to get outside quickly, she hid behind a tall stack of truck tires. She could see the bald man in a gap between the tires; instead of the knife, he held a pistol. She looked around for a weapon, and on the floor nearby lay a tire iron. She reached out, lifted it, and held it close.

Louie walked toward the door, thinking Maddy had run outside. As he passed by, she slammed his hand with the tire iron. The gun came free and slid under the car. Louie reacted by landing a left hook on Maddy's jaw, knocking her almost unconscious. He jumped on her, pinned her arms down with his knees, and pulled out the knife.

"You bitch. You kicked my balls so hard that I can't get a hard-on to fuck you with. So I guess I'll have to do it with a knife." He put the knife to her neck and said, "Don't move, or I'll slit your throat." With his other hand, he started unbuckling her belt. Smiling, he put the knife between his teeth, looking down, trying to lower her trousers. She felt his weight shift, and the pressure on her right arm lessen. She freed it, reached up, grabbed the knife from the guy's teeth, and began slashing at his face.

Louie reeled backward, trying to avoid the blade, and fell, but not before Maddy took a final slash at his throat and struck flesh. He screamed, holding his hands to the wound, preoccupied with his injury.

Maddy knew the wound wasn't severe; the knife hadn't penetrated enough, so she ran to the handgun and grabbed it. She held it to Louie's head, and in an intense, slow whisper, she said, "You killed Adam; now I will kill you."

"Don't, Maddy, don't do it." It was Zep. He was with Hannah and Ethan beside her. Louie stared at the floor, bleeding, as his arm quivered.

At that instant, filled with rage at the man who took the love of her life away forever, she wanted revenge and didn't care what might happen to her. She pulled the hammer on the revolver back; it clicked. She saw Hannah draw her sidearm from the corner of her eye. "Don't make me do this, Maddy," Hannah said. "Put the gun down. He'll get his justice."

"Justice!" Maddy screamed. "What's that? There is no justice, Hannah. This piece of shit will be on the street before I have grandkids." She couldn't believe the word had come out of her mouth. *Grandkids.* She remembered her vision. *Amber will have my granddaughters.* She dropped her head to her chest, turning it from side to side, weeping, and flung the weapon deep into the warehouse.

She got off the man, and Zep ran to her, kneeled, and held her close. Hannah pointed her weapon at Louie as Ethan handcuffed him.

"Oh, Zep, what am I going to do now?" she bawled.

"You're going to go on living and find a way to survive. You're going to keep your head up when it needs to be up and down when it needs to be down," he said, as his voice cracked. "And most of all, you'll keep being your beautiful, wonderful self."

Tires screeched as unmarked cars pulled around the open garage door. Bud and Al ran to where Maddy sat on the floor. "Is she alright?" Bud asked. Someone wrapped his head in a white bandage. A streak of red seeped through, marking the location of his wound.

She felt weakness return as the adrenaline in her body waned; Maddy looked up, put out her hands, and the two men lifted her to her feet. "I'll be okay," she whispered, wiping tears. "I'm going to be okay." With Zep standing next to her, she gazed at Bud and Al.

Al handed her a book. It had green leather with a polished tungsten crest on its cover that said *The Glades.* She took it and, gazing at the source of many sorrows, thought of Kim-Ly. She remembered Kim's question when they visited The Glades Memorial; *Why is the world the way it is?* She looked at Hannah, walked the ledger to her, and handed it over. "It's yours. Make good use of it."

A detective ran to Zep and said a body was in the back of the warehouse. "It's a male." *Oh my God, it might be Adam,* Maddy thought.

CHAPTER 32

It was 4:30 in the morning. With the hospital hallway lights dimmed and the only sound the hum of a vending machine, Hannah's footsteps echoed as she carried a steaming hot cup of coffee and set it next to Maddy. "Have you heard anything?" She said a nurse came out and told her Adam was still in surgery and it would be awhile. She picked up the styrofoam cup and sipped the coffee. The poison still roiled her insides, but the coffee was hot and felt good going down.

The clock on the wall didn't seem to move. She checked her watch, and it was correct; 4:43. More footsteps, and this time it was Zep. When he sat across from Maddy and Hannah, he said he checked on Rose Gilly's condition. "They think she'll heal without limitations, but Nemo Zerilli didn't make it." Maddy asked about Bud, and Zep said he needed a few stitches and had a headache. "He'll be alright."

When Hannah's cell phone rang, she stepped away. Zep asked Maddy if she'd contacted her daughter. "She's flying in today and arrives tonight. My friend Jodi will be here tomorrow."

"You're all welcome to stay with Susan and me. We have plenty of room." She thanked him and said they might take him up on the offer.

When Hannah returned, she found out the DC bureau had already attained warrants for Senator Winthrop, Cynthia Morgan, and five other government officials listed in the ledger. "That document will change many people's lives. We'll track down the women sold at The Glades's auctions and get them the help they need."

When the clock reached 6:04, Maddy stood and stretched her back. She said she needed some air, left Hannah and Zep, and walked to the glass doors in the front lobby. She stepped outside. A few cars moved with their headlights still on, even though the eastern sky was red. She exhaled a deep breath and thought of all that had happened over the past few weeks.

Her mind returned to the night in Washington when she first arrived for the conference. It seemed like an eternity ago. She had spoken with Adam on the phone, and he was tired. When he told her he was going undercover, a pang of worry gnawed at her gut. *Now he is lying on an operating table with surgeons working to save his life.*

She tried to prepare herself for the worst, turned and walked back inside, dreading she might hear the words the night of her father's surgery — *We did our best, but...*

When she returned, Hannah and Zep talked with the surgeon. "Here she comes now," Hannah said. She approached, and her heart pounded. Her stomach tightened as she got close. The doctor looked tired, and she couldn't read his expression.

The tall man dressed in blue looked down at her and told her they had removed the damaged tissue and made accommodations for brain swelling. Maddy felt her legs trembling as he started describing gunshot wounds to the head. Hannah and Zep seemed to notice her distress and moved closer. Hannah held her arm.

"The severity of a head wound depends on the bullet entry and/or exit site. That impacts the areas of the brain damaged. Also, bullet fragmentation and the timeliness of receiving treatment are factors. The victim's age and general health are crucial."

She wanted to know the bottom line. "What are his chances of surviving?" She crossed her arms, feeling her gut in knots.

"If you get shot in the head, this is the wound you want. He's fit; it will help. The bullet was the low-velocity type and traveled well above the base of the skull; that's good. I can't give you the odds of survival; too many things can go wrong. The next few days will tell the story."

Maddy felt Hannah and Zep move even closer; the warmth of their bodies was like a comforting blanket, and their strength was holding her up. She struggled to ask, "Based on the injury's location, what types of disabilities might he have if he survives?"

"If he makes it, he will have problems with balance and maybe his ability to walk." Maddy closed her eyes. *God let him live.* She just wanted to be lying beside him, holding him like she had done the last time they were alone. She asked when she could see him.

"Not until he stabilizes — about four or five days." Then he added, "You should rest and ask the nursing staff to contact you when the time is right."

When he walked away, she didn't know what to do. "Come to my place, Maddy. We'll tell the nurses to contact you there." As they left the waiting area, she felt Adam tugging at her. She didn't want to leave him.

She stopped in the middle of the lobby, tears filling her eyes, and she covered her face as her friends waited before they moved with her outside into the sunlight.

CHAPTER 33

Three years later—July 4th, 1995

Maddy got up early. She made coffee and watched from her kitchen window as fishermen in boats headed to their favorite spots on the lake. The rising sun glittered off The Glades monument, but it was like any other familiar sight, and she paid it little mind. A breeze wafted the herbal, spicy scent of balsam through the open windows, and she took her mug outside to the deck to sit on a step. It had been a glorious summer, and it felt like it might last forever.

The warmth of a tiny body on her right scrunched up next to her. Maddy said, without looking, "Is this Molly sitting next to me, or is this Kimberly?"

"Guess," a little voice said.

"I think it's Kimberly."

"You peeked, Grandma," the child scolded. Maddy turned and tickled her, and Kimberly giggled.

"Good morning, Mom." Amber was in the kitchen. She said good morning to her daughter and told her the coffee was fresh.

"Grab a cup, come outside, and join us."

"Mommy says there are wolves and bears in those woods," the little girl said with a frightened look.

"Yes, but they are too busy raising their babies to be troubled with people. If we let them be, they won't hurt us." Amber walked outside and sat at the picnic table. "How long does Molly sleep?" Maddy asked.

"She loves to sleep late. You'd never know she and Kimberly were twins; there's nothing they do similar." As she gazed at the mountains and the lake below, Amber said, "I'd forgotten what an awesome spot you have. Do you remember the first time we drove here together when it was just an empty field?"

Maddy remembered it well. She had just recuperated from wounds sustained in a shoot-out and wanted to retire from detective work. Building her place on the mountain was her ticket to serenity; it turned out to be anything but.

Molly came outside, rubbed her eyes, and said she had to pee. Amber got up to show her to the bathroom. "Mommy says we're going on a boat today. Are we really, Grandma?" Kimberly asked.

Grandma. The word bounced around in Maddy's head, and she remembered seeing the twins when she wanted to give up and die. "Yes, Kimberly, my friend Lester will take us out on his boat, and we'll go to an island and swim. Won't that be fun? After, we'll visit Rose, another friend. She's made special brownies for Molly and you. Then, Stick will come when it gets dark tonight, we'll make a bonfire, and we'll have fireworks."

"Is Stick a friend too?"

"Yes, he is."

"You sure have a lot of friends, Grandma."

Maddy looked into the child's wondering eyes. "I sure do."

She heard the porch door open. A familiar shuffle followed, and the warmth of another body sat on her left. She turned and leaned her head on Adam's shoulder. "Good morning, babe."

He leaned over and kissed her forehead. "Morning, Maddy."

THE END

ABOUT THE AUTHOR

John spent the early years of his career as a rehabilitation counselor offering a hand to people in need. Some took it, and with them, John was privileged to share their journeys. He learned of real human suffering, the tragedies, and the victories of life. But most of all, he realized we share a never-ending quest to be known. He is dedicated to making his characters known to his readers, even if just a little while. John now writes full time, has published *Cupid, The Glades,* and *The Ledger,* and has plans for several other novels.

DON'T MISS WHERE THE STORY BEGAN!

NOTE FROM THE AUTHOR

Word-of-mouth is crucial for any author to succeed. If you enjoyed *The Ledger*, please leave a review online—anywhere you are able. Even if it's just a sentence or two. It would make all the difference and would be very much appreciated.

Thanks!
John Netti